The SPINSTER'S HOPE CHEST

By Robert W. Spencer

12-26-2018

The Spinster's Hope Chest

ISBN: 978-1-63381-138-6

Designed and produced by
Maine Authors Publishing
12 High Street, Thomaston, Maine
www.maineauthorspublishing.com

Printed in the United States of America

Dedication

To my partner and primary reader, Geraldine

Acknowledgments

The Trustees of the Waterford Historical Society kindly gave me permission to use Berthie Fogg Libby's letter, contained in their archives, as the basis for this story. Without the letter, Lizzie Millett's life would have remained in obscurity.

Many thanks go out to Nancy Marcotte and David Sanderson, who continue to open my eyes to the history of Waterford.

Kathleen Lyman and Maureen O'Donnell's thoughtful comments on the early text pointed me in the right direction; thank you.

Finally, I acknowledge the hardworking men and women of Waterford, Maine, who have given our community such a rich industrial history.

Contents

Foreword: A Discovery

You may be a woman who has been able to make the most of your life after starting off in a childhood of conflict and contrast, or you may be a man who knows such a woman. My heroine, Lizzie Millett, was born into a very troubled world at a time when few opportunities, other than marriage, motherhood, and teaching, were available to young rural females. It was 1861, and yes, there were some women who did not marry. These spinsters might have lived full and satisfying lives assisting with the children of their married siblings, or they might have helped other women through childbirth, but the paths to personal success in a career were almost nonexistent. Hopefully, we are able to say that conditions are different today, though I sometimes wonder.

Three years ago, during a day of volunteer work for the Waterford Historical Society, I came upon a musty pressed-board scrapbook stacked among other such albums in our Town House Museum. With its stained red cover and broken string binding, it barely held secure a collection of newspaper clippings and old photos pasted into its pages by local doyen Flora Abbott during the 1950s. As I leafed through the pages, a small pink envelope with many brown stains slipped out and fell to the floor. It was a personal letter to Flora from her childhood friend, Berthie Fogg Libby, who had moved to California. The postmark was October 10, 1953.

As you will see in that letter, Lizzie Millett was born into a world of many conflicts, both in her family and in the community. The town of Waterford had recently sent many of its young men to fight in the Civil War. The loss of thirty-four men[1*] to battle or disease was a devastating blow to the small community. Lizzie's family was rent with division and hardship: an egotistical father who abandoned his wife and children and a loving mother who died very young. Lizzie's real-life conflicts, the historical facts of my fiction, led her to an unhappy life as a single woman who kept the secrets of these hardships locked in her heart until her death in Westbrook, Maine, in 1948. According to Berthie Fogg Libby, even some success as a dressmaker could not provide her with a happy soul.

While Libby admits that much of her recollections arose from "childhood eavesdropping," hearsay, or rumor, to me the sad story seems believable, though a very, very incomplete summary of her life. I spent much of the next three years looking for the rest of the story and hoping that Ms. Millet might have made more of herself.

1* *History of Waterford, Maine 1775–1875*. Published by the Waterford Historical Society, pp. 203–207.

Introduction:

Berthie Fogg Libby's Letter
(No corrections have been made to spelling or grammar.)

Dearest Flora, I believe they called it the Temple Hill District, and the families I recall were, besides our own Fogg family, the Old Doctor Millett family, the John Baker Family and his daughter Agnes, the Haskells and the Gilsons. The last time I was in Waterford to stop, Harry Watson took Ella Millett Roberts and I up over Temple Hill, and pointed out the old Gilson house, an almost total wreck, which I presume by now is one of Harry Haynes' cellar holes. Josephine Gilson, in my childhood eavesdropping; was an eccentric.

The Doctor Millett family I knew best. I never did know whether he was a doctor to people or animals, but the Waterford History mentions that a Dr. Millet practiced briefly in the eastern part of town. I don't know about the briefly part, but he married Maria Monroe and raised five children there. These were Sewell, Emily, Louise, George, and Ella. Sewell was a handsome, rather dissipated guy, and he paid court to pretty Francena Fogg, much to the dismay of the hard working Foggs. But she married him and after bearing four daughters,[2*] died in her late twenties. She is buried in Bolsters Mills Cemetery.

When Francena Fogg Millett died, the four children became

[2*] According to the 1870 U.S. Census, Lizzie lived in Waterford with her father, stepmother, and three sisters: Cora A., six; Mary M., six; and Hattie, three years old.

a problem. The Milletts, if they were living, did not want to assume their care, and the Foggs had a lot of sickness in their home. The girls ran back and forth between the two houses at will.

Sewell Millett lost no time in finding a step-mother for the children, but when he brought home Rose Haskell as his bride, she either did not want the bother of the older children or the Foggs did not consider her suitable to raise them.

So Grandmother Fogg set about finding homes for Elizabeth and Maria (known as Mamie and later Mollie). She had two sisters who were childless, and presently Lizzie was sent to Bethel to her great aunt, Emeline Dunn, the wife of a wealthy sea captain, and Mamie went to live with another great aunt, Ellen Barker, whose husband was Town Clerk of Bethel for twenty years. Hattie remained with her father, who moved to Oxford, where he and Rose added three children to the Millett clan. When Hattie was ten, Rose left the care of the children mainly to Hattie. I believe she (Rose) went to work in the mill.

When Harriet was about thirteen, my father learned that she had typhoid fever, but was forced to carry the heavy baby about and do much of the housework. He promptly put the old farm horse into the shafts and set off for Oxford. There was undoubtedly quite a scene, and Rose Millett was told a thing or two about the proper care of young girls. At any rate, Hattie was bundled into the wagon and brought to Westbrook looking, as my Aunt Hannah put it, "like a plucked chicken."

If I remember correctly, Mrs. Dunn and Elizabeth did not get along very well, and when Uncle Sam Dunn hanged himself, she asked another sister who lived near us in Westbrook to take the girl. So it was a natural consequence that Elizabeth finally landed with us. She held several jobs, as a weaver in a Saco mill, an employee of the Waltham Watch Co., where she stayed with her aunt Louise Millett Scriber, always returning to Westbrook between times for indefinite periods.

My father operated a stone quarry and got out building stone for nearly all the buildings under construction in those years (1880s). It was his custom to scout around Waterford and

Harrison for sober, steady young men whom he would employ by the year and who lived with the family. In the early '80s, he hired Bert Learned and Henry Green, who were satisfactory. Bert, however, went home to get married, but Henry remained for a second year.

It was during this second year that Lizzie came back from one of her jobs. I do not think that Henry made very ardent court to her, for she was not an especially attractive girl, but Lizzie fell deeply in love. Lizzie began to sew diligently for her hope chest. She really became a different person, for she never had been easy to get along with. Her step was light, her eyes were bright, she sang at her work. From time to time I caught glimpses of a beautiful piece of old rose material which she sewed on in secret, for she was a very secretive person. Henry's year was up, and he said he had a chance to get a farm in Waterford and would not hire out for another year. But he would return for Lizzie when the arrangements for the farm had been made.

Then out of the blue sky, the bolt fell. A letter came from Henry, an eagerly awaited letter. But what news! Henry had acquired the farm all right, the Whitcomb farm, but the consideration was that he take care of the old people, and they wanted him to marry their granddaughter, Ella Whitcomb. And he had.

Elizabeth was stunned. She became an embittered person, and while she put on a brave front days, her pillow was soaked with tears at night. Gradually she accepted her fate, but we were careful not to mention Henry in her hearing. She lived with us for years, building up a dressmaking business, then went on her own.

When she died at an advanced age, Harriet cleared out the accumulation of years, and in an old trunk was the motheaten remains of the old rose dress that had never been finished.

I doubt if Ella Whitcomb Green, who was a very fine person, and a much more suitable wife for Henry than Elizabeth ever would have made, ever knew about the wedding dress that was left unfinished, or the letter that broke a heart. Cordially yours, Berthie Fogg Libby

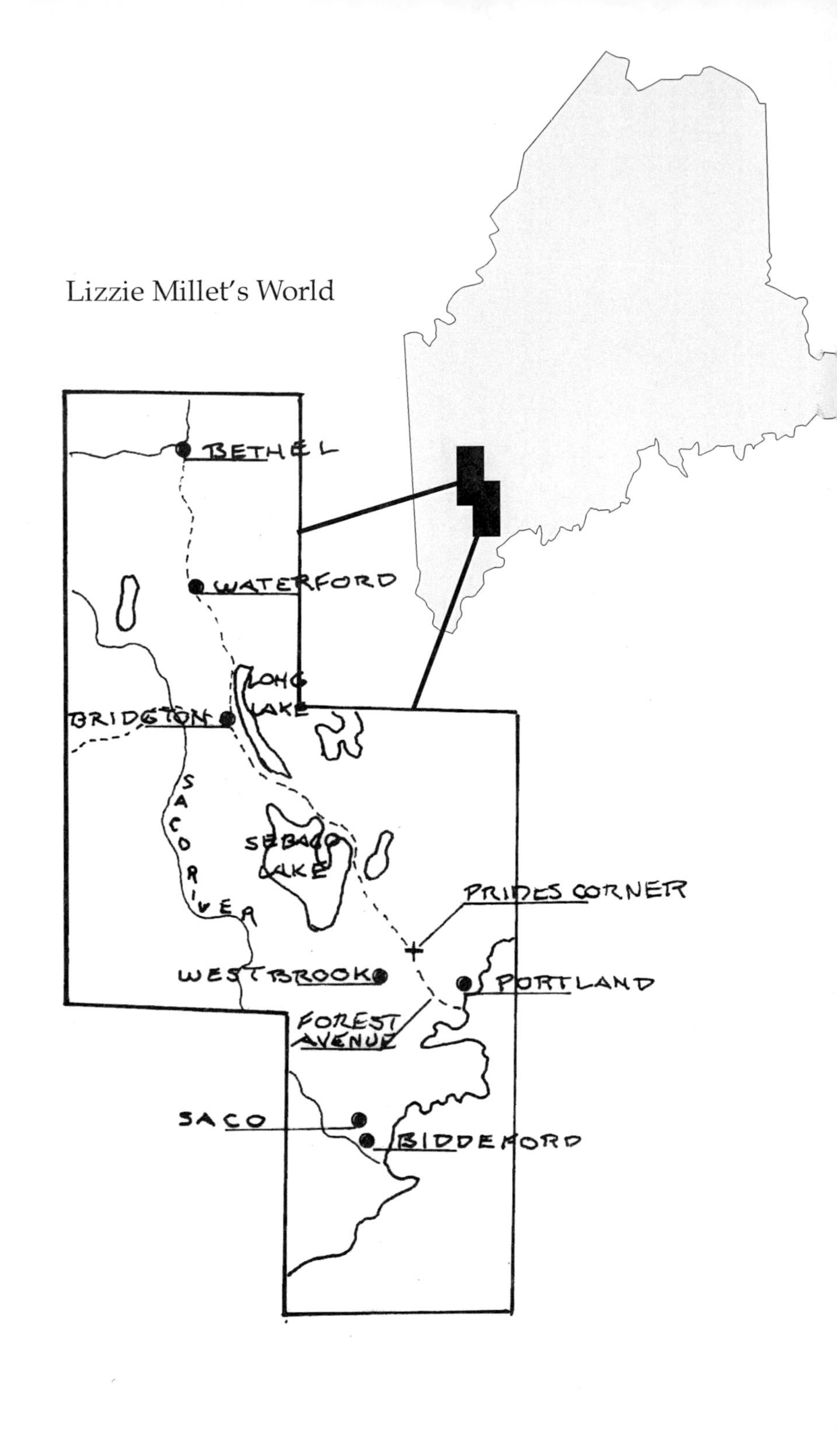

Lizzie Millet's World

Lizzie's Story

1

"I hate you! H-h-hate you! I hate you!" Six-year-old Hattie Millett screamed so loud at her father that her dead mother, whose body still lay in a pine coffin on a table in the center of the parlor, must have surely heard from the other side. The girl waved her arms around as if possessed, screaming and wailing like a banshee.

Her father, thirty-two-year-old Sewell Millett, rushed across the room, grabbed her by the shoulders and shook so hard that one sleeve ripped off her dress. As he was about to hit the girl, nine-year-old sister Lizzie stepped in between. His hand glanced off the taller girl's head, opening a bloody gash just above her ear where his wedding ring struck. The guests at poor Francena Millett's funeral stood in shocked silence. Then two men, the assailant's brother Oren and Hiram Fogg, the girl's grandfather, jumped from their chairs to restrain the man before more harm might be done. Grandmother Beattie Fogg and her daughter Ella each pulled one girl away from the enraged man.

"We both hate you!" yelled Lizzie from behind her aunt. "Hate you and your girlfriend! How could you think to bring her to Marm's funeral? How could you?"

She pointed to Miss Rose Haskell, a seventeen-year-old

neighbor from Deer Hill who had too swiftly stepped in to take the place of Francena in Sewell's life. During the service, she had stood in the rear of the room with his parents. Now she was directly behind her boyfriend with her left hand covering her mouth and her right on his shoulder. The other women in the room stared at the couple and whispered to each other just loudly enough so that their comments were audible to all present.

"How brazen! Shame on both of them! Their families have dishonored the village! Shame, shame, shame."

It was rumored that the two targets of these comments had eloped to New Hampshire to be married in secret even before a death certificate had been filed; but this was only a rumor. Quickly, the widower took Rose's hand and rushed her toward the front door. As they left, he pointed directly at the Foggs. "I shan't return to this house until you have buried her and taken all of her things away. But remember, this is my house, not hers. Be done with your duty as quickly as possible."

2

During the next two days, Hiram and Beattie took it upon themselves to collect Francena's personal belongings for removal to their own home in Westbrook. There really wasn't much to pack—just her sewing baskets, clothes, a few small pieces of jewelry, and several quilts she had made herself. All of these fit easily in a large cedar trunk that Hiram had purchased from a customer of his in Harrison. The trunk was sheathed in tin embossed with an oriental design of leaves and flowers. He had been told that the chest came from China filled with tea leaves. Francena Millett, née Fogg, who had been ill much of her short life, had died in childbirth at the age of twenty-three and lost what would have been her third child. Over the past few years, as Francena's health failed from consumption, she and Lizzie had become equal partners in managing the household and raising young Hattie. The death now left the nine-year-old with responsibilities far beyond her age. While death during childbirth was not uncommon in the 1860s, the loss of a mother, especially for a young daughter, made life very hard.

There had never really been much of a father in the family. Sewell, one of nine children raised by farmer Daniel L. Millett, who was also a doctor, and his wife, Mary Monroe, had more interesting things to do than child-rearing. Other than begetting the two girls with his pale but beautiful young wife, he was hardly ever home, preferring instead to enjoy the unfettered life of a woodsman. As the girls grew, Francena—or "Marm," as they called her—was their mainstay, the glue that held the family together. Her three sisters and Grandma Beattie also shared much of the girls' care, especially as Francena's health failed. Her death brought life up short for the young sisters, regardless of what the others might do for them.

3

After the tumultuous funeral, the Fogg family women gathered in the kitchen around the now cold cookstove. Before leaving Waterford, they wanted to figure out what would be best for Hattie and Lizzie.

"We need to do something quickly. That devil and his hussy will do nothing for them. That is clear. He might even turn them over to the town to live on the Town Farm if we don't come up with a plan," said Beattie.

Her daughter Ella agreed. "No, that just won't do. Then some stranger might adopt them. What if they ended up with the Gilsons on Baker Hill? Heaven forbid. Then they wouldn't even have a proper house to live in. Liz and Hattie best stay in our family. We are the ones who have their best interests at heart."

"My sisters Emeline and Ellen, up Bethel, might provide good homes for them. One in each house, perhaps. They both have successful husbands and are barren. A young one would be sure to bring joy into their lives," Beattie continued.

"Sister Ella," suggested Emy, "you might easily take one more child. Your Ethel could help raise her. It would do the girl some good to have more responsibility than you give her."

"My dear girl, I am sorry, but there are already too many mouths to feed in my house. Especially with William still not recovered from his war wounds. His army pension is some help, but we've had no steady income for years."

Ella glanced at her youngest sister, Louise. She was pregnant again only a year since the last one. Not a likely candidate.

It was then decided that the best course of action was for the grandparents to ride over to Bethel in the morning to see if one of Beattie's sisters would provide the solution needed by the bereaved family.

4

The two girls had possessed in their "Marm" not only a mother, but a teacher and a friend. She had taught Lizzie how to handle household chores like sewing and cooking, and she had taught both girls to read at an early age. Even when they became old enough to attend classes in the schoolhouse close by on Mill Hill, they could learn just as much at home as with the school mistress.

As the sisters matured, the ability to read and write well set them apart from many of their friends. There were always books at home that challenged them. Francena would read these to Liz, who would then learn to read aloud to Hattie. Years after their mother's passing, the two realized that they shared a common recurring dream about those times. Lizzie had first mentioned it in a letter to Hattie.

> *Marm had taught me to read so early in life. Perhaps at three years, I could make sounds of words in books Grammy would bring to me. When I was five, Marm would place us girls high up on the top shelf of her maple secretary desk: the big pine one Grandpa Hiram made for her and was in the kitchen. She always kept an eye on us as she did her chores or her sewing, so that we would not fall. I would read to you,*

Hattie. Or you would make believe to read to yourself, while I might journey on my own to places far away. I could see the places and the people who lived in those little books.

In my dream, I am strapped into the desk with a woolen throw wrapped around my waist, then around you, and tied off tight to the desk with a golden cord. Then, I slip down smoothly from the restrainer. As I begin to fall toward the floor, Marm grabs my arm and tosses me up into the air. I fly high above the kitchen, above our house and out nearly to the stars. It is only at the sound of loud booming, like a cannon, that I wake and fall back safely to land in my own bed.

Without Francena to care for them, the girls were frightened about their prospects. Both realized that Father would do nothing for them, especially after the altercation at the funeral. He had already gone on to his next relationship with young Rose Haskell, who was just eight years older than Lizzie and wanted nothing at all to do with "Francena's little brats," as she called them. She likely would have convinced her new husband to send the girls away to be raised by Millett or Fogg relatives.

While the elders tried to figure out a plan for their well-being, the girls sat on the granite front steps and stared out at the farmland for what was likely the last time. Across the pasture that ran along Temple Hill Road, they spied Farmer Keane driving his horse and buggy past the schoolhouse at the top of Mill Hill Road, where he lived in a house very much like theirs, only quite a bit smaller. In the distance, sunlight shimmered on the rippling waves of Tom Pond. Far beyond the schoolhouse, over in East Waterford, they could make out the end of Long Pond across recently opened pastures.

"We'll not be swimming at our beaches this summer," Lizzie began. "Or playing with the Hamlins on their Bear Mountain farm."

"It just ain't fair, Lizzie, not right we can't stay here and go to school. I don't want to go away. Let's run away. Yes, that's it, let's run away right this instant!"

"Get that idea out of your pretty little head, missy," the older girl admonished. "Grammy, Grampy, Aunt Ellen, and the others: you know they love us. Won't they do what's best for us?"

5

Despite dire expectations, until other arrangements might be made, the girls would stay in the house with Sewell and Rose. It only took a few days of living with the hostile sisters for Rose to realize that she needed to rid the house of them. Most days when the sun was shining, they were up and out of the house before breakfast, either running up to the Hamlin house or all the way down to Bear Pond on the other side of Bear Mountain or Tom Pond, where they might spend all day swimming with their friends. Rose might see little evidence of them for several days at a time, except for muddy footprints in the kitchen or sand all over the outhouse floor.

"Sewell, the tykes are out of control," she said one night when he was at home. "They run free all over the neighborhood at all hours. We don't need the nuisance of her brats messing up our home."

"Rosie, I agree that it would be good to have the sisters sent away. That little one is completely out of control. She won't pay any attention to what I say. Let me speak with the family about getting other homes for them as quickly as possible."

Several days passed before the topic came up again. During that time, Sewell was away and, as was usual for him, had done nothing about the plan. This delay gave Rose time to observe what a good housekeeper Lizzie was. When her husband returned, she had changed her mind.

"The elder girl is very good around the house," she started. "I think it could be valuable to keep her. She is very good at sewing clothes and cleaning. Let's have her stay with us for a time. Without the other girl, she may be easier to manage."

6

Beattie and Hiram spent several days in Bethel, first discussing with her sister Emeline Dunn their plan for her to take Hattie and raise her as her own. Emeline was married to a wealthy sea captain who was away much of the time, and agreed that having a young companion would add new interest to her solitary life. She welcomed the prospect. Sister Ellen Johnson, however, had no interest at all in taking either of the girls. So much of her time was being spent in volunteer work with the Grange and the church, she was seldom at home.

Grandfather Hiram thought that his cousin in Windham might be more cooperative. He had just lost two boys in the war and had plenty of room in his large farmhouse. When, upon returning to their own home in Westbrook, the grandparents learned that Sewell and Rose had decided to keep Lizzie in Waterford with them, the decision was made that Hattie would move to Bethel immediately.

The girls had no say in what was to befall them. The course of their lives was being entirely determined by elders, some of whom were almost strangers. Their desire to stay with their friends in Waterford meant nothing to the adults. Liz dutifully helped the little one pack her few belongings: clothes, two books, and a hand-painted doll made by their Marm. Grammy had even got her a new pair of leather boots from cobbler J.R. Hall in South Waterford for the approaching winter.

"Lizzie, please come to visit me some. I will write to you often." The young one tried to keep from crying. "At least you will be here at home. I am going to some strange place."

"You will be happier than I, dear one. Aunt Emy lives in a big fancy house. Her Captain Sam has filled the place with wonderful things from all over the world. You will have the best life that money can buy. I will be here with a father who cares not a mote for me and a mother who will laze about while I do all her work. We will not see each other for a long time; you can be sure of that."

"I shan't forget you, Lizzie. I love you."

"And I you."

They had never been apart before, even for one day. Now they threw their arms around each other and began to cry. Liz finally pushed Hattie away, wiped the tears from her eyes, and kissed her sister goodbye, not knowing if they would ever see each other again.

7

For the first month or so that Liz lived with Sewell and Rose, she was able to stay out of the house much of the time. Classes at the Temple Hill School just down the road gave her the opportunity to be away during the weekdays. As winter approached, she was late for school some days because she was required to make breakfast for both adults each morning, but only on the rare occasions when Sewell was at home. Other days, she had to leave class early to prepare dinner. She came to hate her weekends, when Rose gave her so much to do that she was unable to spend time with her school friends. Rose would make a long list of household chores for her each Friday and post it on the front of the Hoosier cabinet. Tasks were then checked off on completion. At the end of each day, Rose would review the progress that had been made, and most of the time, Liz was reprimanded for her failures. Completion of the list brought no comments whatsoever.

"Elizabeth, as it is Saturday, you will need to heat water for your father's bath. He will be home from fishing before dinner. There is a chicken dressed and hanging in the barn. You'll need to get that roasted with potatoes before you heat bath water. Now get a move on, or you'll never get everything done on time."

Liz said nothing to this woman who was really but a girl herself. She thought often of running away. Rose didn't even use her real name. I am Lizzie, not Elizabeth, she thought. Is the woman dumb or something? She often thought of going off to Westbrook and letting Grandy and Grammy know how badly she was being treated. They would surely take her in if they knew what a witch

Rose was, treating her like a slave.

Several months after Marm's funeral, Rose had announced to Lizzie that she was pregnant. As the pregnancy progressed, the mother-to-be did less and less in the house. After a new baby girl was born, Lizzie's life became even more difficult. There were days when she could not go to school because care of the newborn was part of her responsibilities. Rose, as soon as she recovered from childbirth, seemed to want no part of the messy work of motherhood. In fact, she often left the house for long visits with her Haskell clan over on Deer Hill. The new mother had absolutely no idea how to raise children, and even if she were taught what to do, it was doubtful she would have been able to concentrate long enough on the tasks at hand to do things herself. She was simply not suited for domestic life.

Sewell, after hanging around to witness the birth of his new child, was seldom home. Although the land inherited from his father had been a successful farm for two generations, he never bothered to husband it. "The granger life is not for me," he often joked. Immediately after the birth, he started a job at a lumber camp in Stow that would keep him away most of the winter. Whenever he was home, he and Rose went to parties or just stayed in the bedroom drinking, smoking, and carrying on. Liz often lay awake at night listening to their loud passionate noises.

One early morning while still in bed, Lizzie heard the two of them shouting at each other in the kitchen.

"Rose, you just had a baby. How can you get another one so soon? What will we do with it?"

"You know how I got this way, for God's sake. You can't leave me alone for a second, the few times you are around. You act like you are a stud and I'm a mare in heat."

"You seem to enjoy it! You are my wife, after all. When I come back from the woods, I need you to satisfy me. That is your job, isn't it?"

"My job, is it? Why the hell don't you just stay back in the woods? Stay there and take care of your own desires for a change. Aren't there some boys there who might satisfy you? Do you think I want to be pregnant again so soon? If I had my way you'd stay away for good!"

Then came the sound of a hard slap and a scream. The door slammed and the woman cried out, "Run, you bastard and never come back!"

Liz knew that caring for another baby was soon to be added to her list of chores.

8

That winter of 1871 went on forever. Rose was sick much of the time and stayed in bed sometimes for many days in a row. Lizzie was glad her father stayed away for such a long time. She had survived more than a year in this horrid situation, she thought, mainly because he was not around to bother her. The first-born, Cora, had grown to become a healthy baby, and even though Liz hated the mother, she showed great affection for her stepsister. The three of them were shut in day after day because of blizzards that came one on top of the other.

Tending the wood-fired range was a constant job for Lizzie. Thankfully, there was a good supply of wood, provided by Rose's father, in the shed next to the barn. Liz had to make sure that, before each storm began, she brought in enough fuel for two or three days. If she didn't, she faced the challenge of going in and out of the rear door without letting snow blow in and heat blow out. After the first series of storms, she learned to judge from the slate grayness of the sky and the wind blowing in from the east that another nor'easter was about to arrive.

One winter day, she went down to the cellar to get potatoes and a squash for supper and noticed that the supply of provisions put up and provided by the Millett and Haskell families had gotten quite low.

"Rose," she said later that day over a simple meal of vegetables and bacon, "I'm not quite sure we have enough food in to make it until spring. Can we get any more from your folks?"

"You would have to ask them yourself. I have not seen anyone from either his family or mine for weeks. Haven't you looked outside? We can't even see through the windows on one side of the house because of the drifts. There have been no wagons on Mill Hill for days."

Liz looked at the weak woman across from her at their small table. This pitiful woman had not been out of the house for a month, and Liz realized that she had to take care of everything in the household herself. Heaven help them if a baby came before spring. The idea that she might have to serve as midwife to this woman whom she hated was frightening. She had seen her mother die even with the assistance of Mrs. Gage, one of the best "birthers" in Oxford County. Spring could not come soon enough.

9

"I'll not have it!" Hiram stormed This good Christian man had reached the limit of his tolerance. "I will not let that hussy ruin Lizzie. Sewell, the bum, does nothing to help. He has that most fertile piece of land and yet his own wife and kids must rely on handouts of food from relatives, while he lives in the woods."

He and Beattie had just received a letter from Berthie Fogg, Hiram's sister, informing them that his granddaughter was being terribly misused. She was so run down with raising the two babies Rose had added to the family that she had contracted typhoid fever. Sewell had not been heard from in many months. Rose, though not yet fully recovered from a difficult birthing, had been forced to take a part-time job as bookkeeper at William Watson's box mill in South Waterford in order to make ends meet.

As they sat over breakfast rereading the letter. Hiram rose and began pacing back and forth.

"What can we do, Hi? She is not our child. Perhaps the Waterford selectmen would find her a home."

"No! No." He cut her off. He was nearly shouting at her, a

thing he rarely did. "This is a family problem. I'll not have her handed off to some other family. We must take things into our own hands. Bea, she already has the fever. Shall we let her die like Francena?"

Sure of what he must do, Hiram stormed from the house, leaving Beattie in tears at the kitchen table. In the barn, he hooked up his Morgan horse to the family cart and took off quickly before his wife could stop him. This would be a long trip in the cool weather, so he wore his heavy winter woolen vest, pants, and storm coat. He carried an oil storm lamp, for he knew they would not return before dark.

On the way to Waterford, a journey of thirty miles, he sang favorite hymns into the wind to keep himself alert. The road was still muddy, so the pace was slow. Maples and birches were budding out in the lengthening spring sunlight, but he spent little time taking in the scenery. In the six hours it took to get there he remained focused on what he must do. By the time he arrived, just after noon, he knew exactly what action to take. As he reached the small gray two-story farmhouse, he saw Rose on her way out the door, returning to work after lunch. He jumped from the wagon bench, meeting her at the gate.

"Hiram Fogg," she said, greeting him with a suspicious smile. "What brings you so far from home on such a spring day? I am out to work, so I can't stay. Lizzie can get you something to eat—that is, if she is awake. She spends so much time in bed these days. I just can't get her to do her chores."

He wanted to slap her. Instead he stood tall and moved forward so she would back up through the gate. She tripped on a loose cobblestone, falling onto dew-damp grass. "Don't strike me!" she shrieked, raising an arm to defend herself. "What the devil has come over you?"

"Rose, if a slap would change you from a dim-witted woman and turn you into a caring mother, it would be a good thing. I won't waste my energy or reputation." He backed away a couple of steps, grabbed her hands, and helped her up from the ground.

"Woman, it is not the devil that has come over me. It is the one that has possessed yourself which draws me here. You and your damned husband have ruined the health of my granddaughter. You treat her as one would treat a slave, make her raise the two babies that you brought into the world but do not want to nurture on your own. You hardly feed her. Her aunt tells me she is nearly dead from the fever. You do not even care enough for her to bring in a doctor."

Rose glared back in his face, her arms akimbo. "'Tis me you blame for this? To hell with you! My bastard husband has left me. He works in the woods for weeks at a time. Sends no money to me. Instead he drinks his pay away. I am left to work six days at the stinking box mill. I come home at night with the smell of sawdust from working in a cloud all day. Even after washing, my clothes reek of wood and grease…but what do you care for my life?"

Hiram put his hands to his ears, not wishing to hear any more of her excuses. He pushed her aside and strode through the open door. Inside there was barely enough light to allow him to see the bareness of the place. As his eyes adjusted, he saw that most of the furniture that had been in the two first-floor rooms during his daughter's funeral was no longer there. He assumed that much had been sold or bartered for food, or burned for heat. To one side of the center stairwell stood a tiny table with two rough-made wooden chairs. On the opposite side, some sunlight was beginning to enter through one small window into what seemed at first to be an empty room. He could barely make out a pair of wooden cribs. At last he spied a small body lying on a tick filled with straw, covered by a light blanket.

"Lizzie, is that you?"

The girl sat upright very slowly, stared in his general direction, and coughed loudly, hand to mouth.

"Yes, 'tis me. Who asks?"

"Girl, I am your Grandfather." He approached the girl, and, bending to hug her, felt her bony shoulders. The heat of her body was feverish. She needed assistance just to stand. He did not think she knew yet who he was.

"Liz, put on your warmest clothes. Pack your belongings in a sack. You are going with me to live with your Grammy Beattie."

Watching from the doorway, Rose said nothing. She walked out the gate and down the path toward her job. She did not seem to understand that her housemaid was leaving and that her babies would be left alone.

Lizzie was soon ready to travel. Her one rough homespun dress would have to do for the trip. Hiram threw a horse blanket around her shoulders. In a burlap sack she had placed several books, two candles, and two old hand-painted dolls. They climbed up to the wagon bench and rode off. As the view of the Millett house faded behind, Lizzie turned to her grandfather and asked, "Who is going to take care of the two babies today?"

On the way out of town on Waterford Road, he stopped the wagon at a spring at the top of Cross Street above the Watson Mill. There, next to the Universalist Church, lived a man he knew well, Mr. J. R. Hall, the shoemaker who had made winter boots for Hattie. As the horse drank from the cool, pure water, Hiram explained to Hall what had just transpired at the Millett place and asked him to relate the same to Mr. Watson, who was a selectman. Perhaps they might arrange to send Rose home for the rest of day, or the town might take the children from her until proper care could be provided.

10

Emeline Dunn was excited about having a child in her home at last. She and Uncle Samuel, or "Captain Sam," as he was known about Bethel Town, had been unable to have a baby of their own, and after fifteen years of trying to conceive, had given up. It was rumored within the family that Sam had a second wife overseas who had provided him with a son. He was said to be away so often, in part, to visit his "island family" in Barbados, where his cargoes of Maine lumber were unloaded. Aunt Emy refused to believe such "vicious rumors whispered behind closed doors" even though she had never questioned him directly about his prolonged absences.

A storage room on the second floor of her Victorian mansion was cleaned out and converted to a girl's bedroom—a fashionable boudoir with curtains of creamy Irish lace, a handwoven multicolored Persian carpet, a four-poster canopy bed, and large bookcases filled with the latest children's books and magazines. Emy had learned from Beattie that Hattie was accustomed to being entertained by her sister, who read stories to her each night before bed and often for hours on end on winter days when school was closed because of storms. Therefore, during the first few months, she made it a point to read aloud after supper each night in the front parlor.

At first Hattie found that her auntie's affectionate company helped soften the sadness of separation from her real family. Reading aloud was enjoyable, even though the books were specifically for young readers and did not challenge her imagination in the manner of more adult works by Stevenson and Twain read aloud by Marm and Lizzie. Perhaps it was the reading style, not the stories themselves, that came to bother her. Unlike her mother and sister, who always took the parts of different characters by altering their voices, Aunt Emy read in a very flat voice and often lost her place, especially later in the evening after sipping her sherry in the afternoon. Hattie also missed the manner in which Lizzie had coaxed her to read on her own, even when the words were difficult. Because she was very proud of her reading skill and wanted to get better with practice, it was annoying that auntie never asked her to read on her own.

"Auntie," said Hattie on one occasion, "you are so kind to read to me each night. It is much like my Marm, sister, and I did when we were together. I do miss being able to read the words myself. Many times there were difficult words I could work out on my own."

"Dearie, your teachers have told me that these books are beyond your reading level. It is best that I read them so that you understand each story."

"Of course, Auntie. You know best," Hattie sighed.

During the rare times when Captain Sam was home, the

house was occasionally filled with neighbors and somctimes foreigners who visited to enjoy elaborate dinners followed by music and dancing in the large dining room with floor-to-ceiling windows. In summer, the room would be lit by the colorful light of a fading sunset. In winter, reflections from gas lamps mounted on the walls would make the snow banks outside shine. After dinner, Captain Sam and other men would pull the tables and chairs out of the middle of the room to make a dance floor. Hattie loved this. She often danced with other children who might be there or even with women friends of her aunt and uncle.

Occasionally, she was asked by the captain to be his partner. He was a short man, so her head stood nearly at his shoulder. They would move in time to waltzes performed by two neighbors who were acclaimed for their skills on violin and accordion. These social affairs were the only times that she could remember Captain Sam being friendly to her and seemingly happy with himself.

She was enrolled in Gould Academy, where lessons were far more advanced than in the common school she was accustomed to in Waterford, but she quickly adjusted. As a country girl, she was usually ignored by her more cultured classmates. When they did pay any mind, it was often to taunt her, asking if she ever went to school barefoot back in "Wattyford." Her ability to read and write brought her good grades and the praise of her teachers, but her intelligence made her even more unpopular with fellow students. The uniforms everyone wore felt too tight on her. She was always getting hers dirty during adventures on the way home. Once, she fell from a tall granite wall, tearing holes in both sleeves and skinning her knees. When she arrived home, Aunt Emy chastised her.

"Hattie, what are we to do with you? You have ruined a brand-new uniform again. I can't keep buying new ones all the time."

She was sent to her room without dinner, thinking how foolish her aunt was. Grammy paid for her clothes, after all, not the Dunns. The thought of her grandparents brought tears to her eyes. This was the first time she had cried since the earliest days after leaving Waterford, and it reminded her of how much she missed her family, especially her sister.

Life in Bethel, which had seemed exciting at first, gradually became more and more unbearable. She had been unable to make any friends, and life at home had turned miserable. Her aunt, who had been so loving and kind, seemed to lose interest in her. There were fewer occasions of reading aloud. The woman often went to bed before dinner, leaving an empty wine bottle on the mantelpiece. Hattie began to make her own meals most nights with whatever ingredients were to be found. The captain was hardly home at all, and when he was there, no one spoke to each other.

When Liz was still living in Waterford, Hattie wrote a series of letters to her letting her know how much she wanted to leave:

> *Darling Liz, I live in the fine big house, as if by myself. Days may pass when I see nothing of Auntie. I feed myself as best I can with whatever is in the larder. Tonight I had an egg from the coop scrambled with butter and a piece of stale bread. My prayers each night are for God to let me be with you once again.*

Liz had written back to commiserate with her, telling her about the cruelty of her own situation before being rescued:

> *My Dear Little Sis,*
>
> *Whilst you feel neglected and unhappy, please apply yourself to making the most of it. You could be here with me scrubbing the skin off your fingers from the cleaning. Rose is a witch. She cares not that I am tired or hungry. Some days I have but an apple or some bread for supper. Meantime, she expects me to raise her two babies, who cry all the time, while she goes off to work or visit with friends. Better that you live in a clean house and can read. My dear, I have not seen a new book in many months.*

The two had been writing back and forth regularly. Then, for several months, Hattie's letters went unanswered, until one came postmarked from Westbrook:

> *"Dear L.S.,*
>
> *I am now freed from my prison and living with Grammy and Grandy in their big boardinghouse. They do keep me so busy helping with meals and sewing for the boarders, but I am so much happier.*

Hattie was relieved that her big sister was once again united with family who loved her. Now, she thought, if that could only happen for me.

Several weeks later, Hattie went early one morning to collect eggs from the coop in the barn. In the damp darkness, she saw a bundle hanging by a rope from rafters near the hayloft. Having never noticed anything like that before, she approached to investigate. To her horror, she saw a man's body hanging there with a noose around its neck. The captain hung like a sack of potatoes. His eyes bulged out. His head was bent over at an odd angle.

Her screams brought Auntie rushing from the house. When she viewed her husband's wretched appearance, her first act was to grab her niece by the shoulder.

"You are never to tell a soul about this. Do you hear me?" She squeezed the girl's shoulder hard and shouted so loudly that Hattie's ears hurt. "Help me get him down. I will untie the rope and lower him down to you. We will tell everyone that he fell off his horse…That's it. It was an accident, not suicide."

Shaking so violently that she could barely talk, Hattie pulled away and ran to the house. It mattered not to her what lies Emy might tell to cover up the sin and cowardice of her husband's demise. However, there was no way she would help with the arrangement of his corpse.

11

When Grandy learned of his brother-in-law's tragic death and the details of the corpse's discovery, he knew at once what his duty was. He set out to Bethel on the family wagon. It had become an all too common journey to rescue a grandchild. Perhaps it would have been wiser to have taken the girls into their boardinghouse after Francena's death. It would have saved a lot of traumatic experiences for everyone, but how could they have foreseen such sad events?

The distance to Bethel from Westbrook, seventy miles, was a full day's journey, so Hiram spent the night at his sister-in-law Ellen's house near Gould Academy. At dawn he put his horse between the shafts and drove across town to Emeline's. He knocked on the front door, but there was no answer. It was early morning, so he was sure Emeline would still be in bed. The girl would likely be getting ready for school. After knocking a second time with the same result, he walked around to the back of the house where it joined the barn. There he spied Hattie in the barn gathering eggs in a basket. She was barefoot and wore a large shawl draped across her shoulders. He was surprised at how thin she had become.

Just then, Emeline came to the back door. She was still in her nightgown, which had fallen open in the front, but she made no attempt to cover her breasts from his view.

"Hiram, what brings you to Bethel today?" Her words seemed slurred, as though she was drunk, but he thought it was because she had just awakened.

"I have come to collect my granddaughter."

"What do you mean? She is mine now, isn't she?"

Hattie came running to her grandfather, threw her arms around his waist, and began to cry. The basket fell to the ground, and several eggs broke on his shoes.

"Grandy! Grandy! I didn't think I would ever see you again! The captain has died. I found him hanging from the rafters right over there in the barn."

Emeline rushed from the doorway, grabbed the girl by her shoulders, and began to shake her hard.

"You little brat! I told you never to tell a soul about this. Never! Never!" she shouted. "Now everyone in the family will know!"

Hiram separated the two and thrust his hand against the woman's shoulder. "Your family already knows what happened. That news is what brought me here. We do not want Hattie to live in such sad circumstances?"

"Then take her. Take her. She has been nothing but trouble for me anyway. She has never appreciated all that I've done for her. Take her out of my sight, for God's sake. I will get her clothes for you."

The woman turned toward the house, but tripped over her own feet and fell on her face. As Hiram stooped to help her up, Hattie ran to the house to gather what belongings she wanted to take. She couldn't believe her prayers had been answered. She was going to be seeing her sister and family once again.

12

Lizzie was up very early that day, rising before the cock crowed. No one else was awake when she put on her cleanest dress and went out to sit on the front stoop to wait for her sister. Nearly two years had passed since they had been together, and in that time, she had shot up over a foot in height and was beginning to bloom into a young lady. Since moving to the boardinghouse, she had been able to return to her sewing. Part of her household responsibility was to make clothes for Hiram and Beattie, as well as herself, and to repair clothes for the boarders. Unfortunately, darning socks, a chore she disliked, was included. But she was into her reading once again, and each evening after dinner, residents might gather in the big front parlor where she would entertain them by reading aloud. She had also returned to school and become an A student.

The noise of a wagon approaching from the west broke the

predawn stillness. A flock of mourning doves fluttered up from their pecking in the driveway as it entered. Jumping up from the step, Liz saw Hiram in the seat, but no sign of Hattie. When the wagon came to a full stop she ran out shouting, "Grandy! Grandy!"

"Hush, girl, hush!" He held his index finger to his lips. "You'll be waking our little Hattie and spooking the horse."

Hattie lifted her head from where she had been sleeping behind the seat. As she stood and wiped her eyes, Liz saw that her little sister was much thinner than when they had last been together in Waterford. Her hair was quite long, her face very pale. When Hattie caught sight of her sister, she quickly smoothed her dirty blue dress, then lost her balance in her excitement and nearly fell off the wagon. Hiram grabbed her arm and lowered her to the ground.

"Lizzie! Lizzie!" she shouted. "I've waited so long to see you again. How pretty you are!"

Liz threw her arms around Hattie, nearly squeezing the life out of her and lifting the small girl off the ground. "You are the dearest thing in the world to me, Little One. I will never let you go away from me again."

13

For nearly thirty years, Hiram Fogg had run a stone quarry in Westbrook located at Pride's Corner on Forest Avenue, near the Windham line. During the early years, he worked with a crew of local lads to cut slabs and blocks of granite from huge boulders that sat above ground in locations where they had been dropped by glaciers thousands of years before. The area around the stone yard was littered with many such boulders; most were as big as a man. Others, known as "glacial erratics," might stand as large as a house. When a large stone was to be processed, a team of two steady men drilled a line of boreholes on a line drawn on the rocks surface according to the size of the slab required. One man held an iron rod with a star bit at one end on the line and waited for the other to strike the butt end of the rod with a ten-pound sledge. Over and over the rod was hit. Once the holes were cut, pairs of iron feathers and wedges were inserted and driven into the stone with a heavy hammer until the stone split close to the line. Such strenuous work required a steady hand, a strong back, and trust between team members that the sledge man would not hit the rod holder.

When the war came, business slowed to a snail's pace as most of the best men in the community signed up for service. At war's end, Hiram expected to be able to step up production with a larger crew. However, he continued to have a difficult time finding steady, sober young men to do the heavy physical work.

It was now 1879, more than a decade since the surrender at Appomattox Court House; yet so many veterans who had returned continued to live with injuries of both body and mind. It was easy to identify a handicapped man who might not be able to handle sledges, star drills, feathers and wedges, or operate a hoist to lift split slabs onto ox-drawn wagons for delivery. A drunk was different. Often the drunkard might seem to be a good worker and might be hired, but he would soon prove to be a laggard who might not show up on some days, and when on the job, might make life more dangerous for the steady men. Even more of a waste for Hiram was the time taken to bail a hungover worker out of jail on a Monday morning.

The Foggs turned their large home into a boardinghouse where contracted workers could live. This allowed them to keep a closer eye on the crew members and provide a bit of extra income from room and board. Hiram spent many hours in Westbrook and Windham, as well as in Harrison and Waterford where he had customers and contacts, looking for reliable men who would sign on to mine for a year and board with his family. With the two sisters united under their roof, he and Beattie began to feel more confident in taking on more than the two workers that had been the norm for several slow years. More hands could make for more production. The girls most certainly took some of the pressure off of Hiram and Beattie, both of whom had begun to feel stressed by the enormity of their business as they entered their sixties.

Once reunited, the sisters took over the chores of running the house. Liz, who had already been sewing and doing the laundry, assumed most of the cooking chores under the tutelage of her grandmother. Hattie, although not quite as proficient at housekeeping, ironed and cleaned. They were a godsend to their grandparents. Together, the girls entertained the boarders each night, reading aloud the stories of Robert Louis Stevenson and Mark Twain. The stories of Uncle Remus by Joel Chandler Harris often regaled all parties until it was time to retire. The two readers themselves had great interest in W. D. Howell's *Lady of the Aroostook* because Lydia, the leading character, had risen from a broken home, just as they had, to become a famous opera singer. Oftentimes the girls brought the roles of various characters to life by acting out the parts. Hattie drew much applause for her enactment of Br'er Rabbit, and Lizzie's playing of Tom Sawyer was repeated many times on request.

Hiram's business had grown rapidly as the economy began to rebound after the war years. Increased demand and improved quarrying techniques made it possible to cut away sections of exposed ledge rather than being limited to odd-shaped glacial boulders. He was now supplying stone for building projects throughout Cumberland and southern Oxford counties. With the railroad now running regularly from Portland to Boston, he faced the prospect of a widely expanded market.

As the years passed, both Lizzie and Hattie took over more and more of the responsibility of running the boardinghouse, to the point where Beattie was able to do something she had wanted to do for years: garden. Although their lot was not large enough to farm, she turned the entire sunny rear yard into beds where she grew produce for the kitchen. The girls often leant a hand in planting, weeding, and harvesting, but for the most part, this work became their grandmother's main contribution to running the business of the house. Boarders now numbered from four men in the winter months to as many as seven during the busiest times. All took a shine to the girls, who brought so much light and life to the accommodations. The young men of marriageable age often developed crushes on one or both sisters, which led to many interesting squabbles between both sisters and suitors. The older quarrymen, either war veterans or fathers with families of their own, doted on them as they would their own daughters.

At seventeen, Lizzie had blossomed into a flourishing young woman who was competent in all the skills needed to run both a household and a business. She took over keeping the ledger for Hiram, freeing him to enjoy a bit of leisure time. She was five feet eight inches tall with a fine full figure that drew a lot of attention. Like her late mother, she was, by her own admission, quite plain of face; but, also like Marm, her lack of outward beauty was more than balanced by an inner beauty that gave her a mysterious allure. While boarders often tried to share time with her, she sensed that they might be out to take advantage of her. Several instances brought back memories of her father's crassness and cruelty.

Hattie, though only fourteen, had developed into a real beauty who never failed to stir the interest of the men whenever she entered a room. The Foggs often had all they could do to keep the more persistent young men safely away from her. One of the more industrious young workers, Nathan Hallett from Windham, became enamored with her as soon as he was hired. He never missed an opportunity to sit close to her at dinner or to help her carry dry laundry in from the line. He even began to play a part in the evening readings so that he might win her smile.

One day, Nathan approached Hiram in the quarry just before the workday ended.

"Sir, Mr. Fogg, do you have a moment to chat?"

"Yes, Nathan, but please use my Christian name, Hiram."

"Yes, sir, Hiram. It is about your granddaughter Hattie. She is such a wonderful girl."

"She is that, and more. With her sister, she is running the house now. So talented. They both are the reason Bea and I have been able to have a bit more free time recently."

"Hiram, sir, I am very fond of her. In fact, I would like to ask for her hand in marriage."

Fogg stared at the boy in disbelief. Here was the youngest man on his crew—just eighteen years of age—asking for permission to ask his fourteen-year-old granddaughter to be his wife! My god, he thought, these are only children, especially Hattie. Yes, she is strong and very beautiful, but certainly not prepared to run a household or, heaven forbid, to have babies. He was speechless.

The handsome young man continued to smile and held his hand out as if to shake on the agreement. When no response was forthcoming, he dropped his hand and asked again, as if the man had not heard his first request.

"Please, Hiram, consider my request to marry Hattie. I am very serious. You know that I am a good and smart worker. You know that my family has more than two hundred acres under improvement in Windham and that we are very well respected in the community. I am surely able to offer her a good life."

"Nathan, I do not doubt your ability to care for her. However, you must admit that you both are quite young to strike out on your own."

"Sir, I am nearly nineteen and have proven my maturity both at home on the farm and here in your own quarry. Please, do not doubt me," he stated.

Hiram could see that the lad was offended.

"Yes, you are correct. I apologize for questioning your worthiness. Hattie, however, is the one for whom I have the most concern. I will speak with her grandmother about this matter this evening and will talk more with you tomorrow."

At the large supper table that evening, Nathan was unusually quiet. Hattie, sitting across the table from him, tried in vain to strike up their usual cheery conversations about the day just past. She smiled at him and tried to get him to look at her and smile back. She couldn't understand what had come over him. Her grandfather also was very quiet, seeming to be deep in thought about some problem unknown to the others.

At the end of the meal, as Hattie and Lizzie cleared and washed the dishes, Hiram whispered to his wife. As the others gathered in the parlor to smoke and wait for the evening's readings, the Foggs exited the house and sat alone on the front porch.

Hiram could have predicted Beattie's initial reaction to the news.

"Hi, she is still so young—such a baby, really. Francena was just fourteen when we gave her to Sewell. He ruined her. I don't want that to happen again."

"She's no longer a child, Dear. You see how the men are drawn to her like iron to a magnet. This boy comes from a respectable and prosperous family. Seems to be a good worker and will likely be a good provider for her."

"Yes, yes… I'm sure you are right. But I just can't see her pregnant at fifteen, like her mother. Yes, I know we saw so many young mothers in the times before the war. But it was different then, with everyone living on the farms and wanting a large brood."

"I know. Having children at such a young age was very bad for Francena. Yet Hattie is much healthier than her mother. Now, you have to admit that."

After sitting in silence for a few moments, considering the wisdom of his words, Bea said, "Hi, I can agree with you about the engagement, but only if they wait for a year before the wedding."

"Bea, we both must speak to them as her parents might have. The young ones always have a problem with waiting for anything."

14

Informed of the grandparents' decision the next day, Nathan went immediately to Hattie, who was reading on the parlor settee.

"Hattie, I want to ask you a question." He reached for her hand and a wide smile spread across his face.

"Well, that is the smile I waited for at dinner last night, but you were so unfriendly. What is going on?

"Will you marry me, Hattie? I love you so much and want to be with you the rest of my life."

Hattie stared at him. "Oh, Nathan! Are you crazy? You want us to get married?"

Putting his arm around her shoulders, he leaned in to give her a kiss on the cheek. She did not withdraw, though her response was far from affectionate.

"Have you talked with Grandy about this? He and Gram are the nearest thing to parents I have. How do they feel about this?"

"Dear Hattie, the reason I was so quiet last night was that I had spoken to Hiram and was waiting for him and Beattie to discuss my wish to wed you. Although they have reservations, they have given their approval."

It was her turn to take his hand and place a tender kiss on the back of his fingers. She had been enjoying his company more and more each day and had hoped that they might someday be together. That it would happen so soon was beyond her dreams.

"Yes, dear Nathan, I will marry you."

After he left, Hattie rushed to her sister and announced with joy that she was to marry Nathan. Liz, she feared, would be sorry to lose her as a constant companion. Her older sister seemed to share the same concerns as the elder Foggs.

"Dear Hattie, are you ready to take this man as your partner for the rest of your life? You both are so young."

"Yes, I am young. So is Nathan, though four years older than I. It does give me pause to take on a woman's responsibilities. I have learned much from you and from Grammy. Still..."

Liz interrupted. "If you fear that you may fail, it is not the time to wed. If you feel that he will expect you to be perfect, then he also may not be ready. If you love each other and can be patient enough to let each other grow, then you will be all right."

Such words of wisdom coming from a woman of her age showed how mature Liz had become despite—or perhaps because of—the early hardships and grief she'd endured. Her advice also reflected the caution with which she judged a relationship between a man and a woman.

"Yes, we do love each other. He is a sweet lad. He says that his mother will be kind to me and will welcome us to live in her house. He says that she promises to help me in the household duties as she is able. His father, as you may know, never came back from Gettysburg, so she has run the farm herself with Nathan's assistance until he came to work here. His brother Thomas also helps out some, but he has his own place in Gorham. The three of us will likely make a good team."

"Little Sister, I will sorely miss you."

"And I you," Hattie said, reaching out to hug Lizzie.

"You will have your own life to live away from me. Your plans seem wise. That must be from the wisdom Marm taught us long ago."

"Yes, Lizzie, I have been thinking about her life so often these last few days. She married at my age also. And she was so unhappy."

"Hattie, the times today are different. Years ago, men and women married not for love but by arrangements made for them by others. Now we know that love can overcome many obstacles. You will make a good mate for that boy and he for you."

Hattie sensed that, within these words of acceptance and encouragement, her sister was masking personal doubts about her own future without her sister around for support. Indeed, the elder girl felt a deep longing to seek a life away from the boardinghouse, a life where she might find the right man and raise a family. Her younger sister surely would be happy, and she wanted to be happy, too.

15

The following Sunday, Beattie took both Hattie and Nathan aside after dinner. The three sat on the wide steps of the front porch facing busy Forest Avenue.

"Children, Hiram and I are pleased that you agreed to delay your wedding for a year. You know that we are both concerned with Hattie being only fourteen. Hattie, you have also questioned whether or not you are ready for the responsibilities of running a household and raising a family."

Both young people started to speak at the same time. Hattie demurred to Nathan so that he spoke first.

"Mrs. Fogg—er, Beattie. You know that I am almost nineteen, not a child any longer."

Beattie responded, "Yes, you are a man in everyone's opinion. Your mother has agreed with the match. Hiram says you are one of his most responsible men. I am sure you are ready. It is Hattie with whom I have a concern."

Hattie reached out to touch the back of Grammy's wrinkled hand. "You are so dear to me in your concern. I understand it. Please believe me that during the year we wait, I will prepare for life with my husband in every way. I will work harder than ever to learn all the skills it takes to run the house. You and Lizzie will be my teachers."

"Of course," said Beattie, "you can count on us to work on that. There is, however, one area in which we may not be able to provide adequate lessons. That is the matter of sex."

Hattie and Nathan were taken aback by the elder woman's openness. While they had shared many passionate caresses already, the topic of their sexual relationship was so personal that the idea of another person being interested, especially an old woman, made them blush.

Again, Nathan was the first to speak.

"Beattie, I am deeply in love with Hattie. To have her as my mate is a desire that grows stronger each minute we are together. Be assured that I can and will control myself. Respect for her and her family will be much stronger than my desires."

Hattie noticed tears forming in her grandmother's eyes. Once again she reached out to rub Beattie's hand. This time her fiancé took hold of both women's hands. There was a long silence before Hattie finally spoke.

"I know that you fear the same fate as befell my mother might come to me. That is in my mind, as well. After he and I are wed will be the time that we will try to make a baby."

16

During the next year, Beattie, Lizzie, and Hattie threw themselves into preparing the younger sister to run a household. She learned cooking, cleaning, and gardening from her grandmother, bookkeeping and sewing from her elder sister. Beattie educated Hattie in the facts of life as best she could. After all, many years had passed since she had counseled Francena, and she was not sure that she had done a good job back then. She taught Hattie that there were certain times of the month when it was best to refrain from having sex because of the increased chance of pregnancy. She was to keep track of the full moon and record her period each month. Hopefully, the young bride would follow these instructions.

Nathan, besides doing the work for which he had been hired at the quarry, showed a great willingness to pitch in and assist his new family, helping Hiram maintain the house and process firewood from the woodlot. Nathan's mother, Eunice, often came to visit on Sundays so that she could get to know the Foggs and be in on the wedding plans. She offered the use of her large home in Westbrook for the service and reception as an alternative to the crowded rooming house. Though it was likely all the boarders would be attending the wedding, the elegance of a Victorian farmhouse was a welcome idea to the engaged couple.

June twenty-seventh was set as the date for the wedding. As was the local custom, the marriage was a simple service in the formal parlor of the large house. Vases of flowers—long-stemmed roses, peonies, gladiolas, and daisies—stood at each floor-to-ceiling window. A regal red carpet runner ran from the driveway up the gravel path to the front door and on into the parlor. The exterior of the Victorian was festooned with red, white, and blue crepe and American flags in preparation for the upcoming holiday.

Liz and Beattie both served as bridesmaids, and Hiram gave the bride away, just as he had done for Francena many years before. As he and the bride walked across the room on the red carpet toward Nathan and his brother, Grandy felt as proud as if he were the bride's real father. In the lovely linen dress and lace veil made by her sister, Hattie looked much older than her fifteen years. At least, so it seemed to Liz, who wept openly to see her beloved "Little Sister" become a married woman. She wished the young couple great happiness and success, though at the same time, she prayed that they would delay starting a family. Hattie was very healthy, to be sure, and Nathan seemed to dote on her completely. However, there remained a fear that early pregnancy might hurt their prospects for happiness as it had for their mother.

Following the ceremony, Widow Hallett provided all with a festive reception of stylish canapés and flutes of French champagne. For most of the guests who lived a more rural lifestyle, such flair and fashion was exotic, nearly European, but certainly very enjoyable.

17

Nathan adored his new wife. He wanted to make sure that she had the best of everything, so he started by taking her to Boston for their honeymoon. His mother and the Foggs had been very generous, enabling them to splurge. They stayed in a suite at the Parker House on Tremont Street, just across from the recently completed City Hall. It was supposedly the same room in which Ralph Waldo Emerson had stayed several times. Hattie was intrigued because Emerson had also spent much of his youth in South Waterford near the place where she was born.

She had never been to Boston, so the excitement and novelty of their trip by rail from Portland had both stimulated and tired her. Nathan had been to the city one time before when he had accompanied his father on a business trip just after the war. At that time he had stayed in the same establishment, a memory which led him to select it for this trip.

"Nathan, Nathan, what a marvelous place!" Hattie began as he lifted her over the threshold into their room. She wore a dark tweed travel coat over a pale-green taffeta dress with long sleeves and a lace collar. Lizzie had taken such pride in presenting this most modern European-style outfit to her after the marriage service.

"I feel like a princess in a castle. Where are my ladies-in-waiting?" She laughed at her own words as Nathan kissed her cheek and set her down on a window seat atop a brocade cushion.

"That is exactly how I want you to feel today and every day, my queen. You deserve to have a better life ahead of you than you have had in the past."

They had discussed all the troubles of her early life, and her stories had cut him to the quick, so much so that he wanted to protect her from hard times in the future. He was by no means a wealthy man, though his father had bequeathed a generous estate to him and his mother. With these resources he vowed to make a happy life for his new wife. As a uniformed bellhop carried the luggage into the room, Hattie removed her travel bonnet, allowing her long brown hair to cascade in curls. She was so attractive in the sunlight that came through the window that the man, who stood waiting for his tip, could not help but stare.

Nathan pressed several coins into the bellhop's hand and said to him, "You'll not see a girl so beautiful in all of Boston or anyplace else, I'd say."

18

In 1880, Fogg hired two Waterford men, Bert Learned and Henry Greene, who worked out well for him. Bert had grown up on a farm in North Waterford and had worked in several sawmills there. He was used to hard work. Henry was from South Waterford, where he had been raised by his widowed mother following the war. He was a quiet boy, but very smart, and stayed to himself most of the time. It was late in the season to be taking on new men, but business had been very good, and with Nathan having left his employ, Hiram needed a replacement. Good quarrymen and honest, clean, churchgoing roomers, both new hires not only proved to be good workers, but also fit quickly into life at the boardinghouse, spending many evening hours in the parlor with the family. Now that Hattie had moved away to Windham with Nathan, Lizzie alone read aloud to them and the others. She also began to tutor Henry on his writing skills. For the nineteen-year-old Lizzie, it was a great pleasure to entertain two handsome young men along with gnarly old war veterans, some old enough to be her own father. Most evenings, the older boarders retired early after dinner, leaving her alone with the two new men from Waterford.

Bert had a girlfriend back in East Waterford, so he made it clear to Hiram that, after the first year, he planned to return to marry her and work her family's farm, which as an only child she had inherited at the death of her father. Henry was free of any such commitment, and Lizzie began to take a shine to him, although he was five years older than she. After he signed on for a second year, they began to spend more time together apart from the rest of the household. It didn't really seem to Grandy that they were courting, but they did get along quite well. Henry, being quite a handsome man, was looking for a wife who was a beauty. Liz was not his ideal, but she would make any man a good housewife with her many skills. The clothes that she wore, all hand-made, were very stylish and showed off her curvaceous figure very well. His eyes would often follow her movements as she hung clothes out to dry, and on evenings when she read to him and the others, he might lose track of the story, concentrating instead on the rise and fall of her chest as she read.

Beattie took notice of the attention given to Liz by Henry and spoke with Hi about the new man.

"There is something strangely familiar about the way Mr. Green treats our Liz. Seems that she has become quite friendly with him, and I don't want to pry into her business, but he doesn't seem to me to be her type."

"Bea, he's just a quiet man. Perhaps they will get on well,

perhaps not. Let's just let them be."

"I know, I know, but I just don't want to see her get hurt."

One Saturday afternoon, Liz and Henry walked alone to the orchard to select apples for the Sunday dinner pie. Henry climbed up onto the lower scaffold branches and plucked fruit, tossing each apple down to Liz, who quickly filled a willow basket. The sun shone brightly at the start, but a dark towering thunderhead soon popped up. Rain began to fall amidst a rash of boomers and lightning. The two ran quickly toward an icehouse just off the barn. Ducking inside the heavy oak door, they turned and watched apple branches wave in gusting winds. Overripe fruit fell like giant hailstones into the unmown grass.

Each felt the other's warmth in sharp contrast to the chill that radiated from the remaining blocks of lake ice still buried in layers of sawdust nearly eight months after being sawn and stored.

"Let me hold that basket for you, Liz. It must be a bit heavy." He reached for the handle.

"Henry, you are so considerate. It really isn't too heavy, but the handle is rough to my hands."

As she transferred the basket to him, their hands brushed lightly together. Both pulled back, allowing the basket to tumble onto the cold ground. As they laughed and bent down to gather the apples from the damp sawdust, Henry gazed at her. They had never been so close to each other. Yes, she was not a beauty, but her body did appeal to him. He reached out to touch her arm as she returned several fruits to the basket.

His touch was warm to her bare skin. While it would have been more proper to pull back, she moved closer until they were face to face.

"Henry, I hope you don't find me shameless in saying that I enjoy being with you."

"No, I feel the same about you, Lizzie. You have been so kind to me these last two years. When we are together in the evenings after supper, your reading has helped to show me worlds and thoughts that I have never before known. I want to thank you for that."

He drew her face up closer and kissed her forehead gently.

"I take that as a thank-you kiss." She smiled up at him, then raised up on her tiptoes and kissed him firmly on the lips. It was something she had never done before. A shiver of passion spread through her. She wanted more. Yet her feelings confused her.

"That is my 'you're welcome.'"

They withdrew from each other for a moment. Then he reached out to hold her hand. She took his arm and placed it around her waist. Later, as the sun burned through the storm clouds, they slid the heavy door away and walked back toward the house, both keenly aware that their relationship had changed.

19

In the following weeks, Beattie noticed that Liz and Henry spent much more time together. The after-dinner readings continued as before, but he often sat closer to her than the rest and turned the pages for her. Then, occasionally, when the girl was spinning her thread, he would lend a hand by holding the wool rolags and feeding them into the whirring wheel. They often went out to the orchard together on Sundays after church to gather apples for the butter and sauce that Beattie was putting away for the winter.

One work day morning, after the men had gone to the quarry, the two women sat over a pleasant cup of hot cider.

"Liz, girl, I see you are enjoying the company of that young man. Has he expressed any interest in your company?"

"No; he is so reserved. I try to bring him out of himself and let him know I like him. Gram, he is such a kind and considerate boy with great plans for his future. He wants to buy a farm and settle down. That is really the only topic of discussion that excites him. I do like our time together. He seems to like me, though he is a bit on the shy side."

"Shy is good, girl. It is a good trait in a man. Your grandfather was also quite that way when we first met. When we were together, though, he would always warm up. He talked more to me than anyone else. Perhaps that is one of the things that drew me to him. That and the fact that he is so handsome. Your friend is also quite a handsome one. Or perhaps you haven't noticed."

Liz blushed and sipped the cider. "Yes, oh so handsome. I could look into his eyes for hours." She stopped herself from going on about Henry, afraid that she was revealing too much.

"Could you look into those eyes for years?" asked Beattie.

20

The men returned to the boardinghouse late that night, as they would for the next few nights. As winter approached, there was much work to be done drilling lines of boreholes in the granite ledges. It was tedious work that prepared blocks and slabs for splitting in the spring after winter ice froze in the holes and helped to split the stone. When they returned each night, Beattie and Lizzie had a late dinner prepared for them. There was little time for conversation and little interest in such on the part of the tired quarrymen.

When Sunday came, Henry had a chance to approach Liz and her grandparents with exciting news. First he spoke with Liz as they walked out to the orchard.

"I received some good news in a letter from Bert today. His wife wrote it for him. He is settled on his farm. She is pregnant with their first now. He seems very happy. Also, he tells of a farm, the old Whitcomb place in West Waterford, that is up for sale now. The farmer and his wife are along in years, and they have no children who are interested in it. It is likely a run-down old place, but he says the soil is good, and there is a strong stand of timber that might turn a profit early on. I've a mind to buy the place."

"Oh, what good news! Do you know farming? Could you make a go of it?"

"Yes, I think so. When I was young, my mother would send me to live with my uncle in Brownfield. He had a small place, but big enough to give me a list of chores to do every day during the summers. Anyway, if I need help in learning the ropes, there is always the Bear Mountain Grange. They give lessons for animal husbandry and farming, you know."

He hesitated for a second. His excited voice quieted. "The Grange also provides instructions for wives in skills of household management—cooking, budgeting, sewing, those types of things."

"But," she said, "Would you be taking a wife with you to the farm?" Her mind was set in commotion with thoughts of his good fortune and what it might mean for her own future.

"Dear Lizzie, if I go to Waterford and buy this farm from the farmer Whitcomb, I would not go alone. With a good wife by my side, I am sure we could make a good life in that country place."

He said this so hesitantly that she sensed a reluctance to even ask her the next question. Perhaps it was that shyness again. If she took it upon herself to speak, she would be taking a risk in being so forward, but she was sure that he felt the same way she did about their shared future. It was just his shyness that held him back.

"My dear sweet Henry." She grabbed his arm and pressed his hand to her lips. He, in turn, put his other arm around her, drawing her very tightly to himself. She said quietly, "It would be so much to my liking to live with you for the rest of my life. Yes, I will marry you!"

Henry said nothing at first, but stared at her in surprise. She thought that she had made a terrible error in assuming that he wanted to marry. Perhaps he had another woman with whom he wanted to spend the rest of his life. But at last he smiled, put his hand on his heart, and knelt in the grass in front of her.

"Forgive me, Lizzie, for not having the courage to ask for your hand. The thought has been on my mind, but I was afraid that you would refuse me."

He rose from the ground and put both of her hands around his neck. Then they shared a long, deep kiss that lit her passion to boiling. Never had she thought there would be such a young and handsome man who might sweep her off her feet and commit to marriage. She was ready to go with him to a new life like the one her sister was enjoying. For the longest time, they stood pressed together, both of his arms wrapped around her. Kisses came one upon the other until their breathing quickened. Henry loosened one arm and began to caress her bodice. At first she drew back. Then her passion took control. She felt his manhood swell against her belly.

At last, Lizzie gently pushed him away so that she might catch her breath. He caught her up again and, lifting her off the ground, kissed her breasts through the fabric of her dress. His hand began to explore beneath her dress and into her knickers. Once again she pushed him away, this time with all her strength. They looked closely at each other.

"Lizzie, let's celebrate by making love right here in the orchard. We will be married soon anyway."

"No, we must wait. I will not give myself completely until after the wedding. You must get permission from Grandy and Gram. They are, for all practical purposes, my parents. With Mother long dead and Sewell long gone, they have given me a good life."

As they walked back toward the house, she smiled up at him and said, "There's one thing I'll not need the Grange to help me with. I'm sure my sewing is far better than those women who might be the teachers."

21

In the days following Henry's departure for Waterford, Liz felt renewed happiness in her life. Not that she had been unhappy before, living in Westbrook with her grandparents. No, she was forever grateful to them for their love and care in the nine years since they had rescued her from that dreadful life in South Waterford. In their busy home, she had grown from a twelve-year-old waif to a grown woman who could read and write well, take complete care of a household, and handle farm work to boot. Over the past few years, as clothing styles became more varied, she had even begun to take in work as a seamstress and dress designer for family members and neighbors, using patterns available through women's magazines.

There was some trepidation in the thought of having to return to her old hometown, of a chance meeting with Rose Millett or perhaps even her father. But she realized, as time went on, that the strength she might draw from a good marriage, as well as the long years of loving care from her grandparents, most certainly would enable her to weather any such storms. After all, there had been no contact with Sewell for many years. She had heard that he'd lost his job in a local carding mill because of a drinking problem and moved away to New Hampshire, where he had taken up with another younger woman. According to Aunt Berthie, who wrote often, Rose now lived in Oxford and had married another man with whom she had brought two more children into the world.

Nathan, who occasionally traveled to look for cattle and horses for the farm, had recently stopped in at the boardinghouse on his return trip. He had heard news of both Rose and Sewell and reported to Lizzie.

"Several men in Harrison told me that your father was in very ill health. They thought he might not live too much longer. The drinking and carousing has caused problems with his stomach and nerves."

She held up her hand to stop him. "I don't care to know more about the man. It has been years since I stopped thinking of him as my father."

"Hattie, too, has given up on him. She will likely tell me to keep my news to myself. Do you wish to know more of Rose, or have you crossed her off your list as well?"

"Best that I hear nothing about that witch. She made my life miserable enough to last a lifetime. As with Sewell, when I hear of them, it dredges up memories of which I have no need."

Hattie often visited, and one day she arrived with some very important news. Immediately upon entering her sister's sewing room, she nearly shouted, "Liz, I am pregnant! Nathan and I are so excited. We both want to have a large family."

"Such wonderful news, Little Sister! Have you told Grammy

yet?

"No. I'm afraid she will not be happy with me. She and Grandy did want us to wait longer. I know they fear that such an early pregnancy might be unhealthy, but I just couldn't wait any longer."

Although Lizzie shared some of her grandparents' fears, she couldn't help but share her sister's joy.

"You are so happy! She will see that and welcome the news."

"Nathan is so good to me. Makes me feel like a queen. His affection and love are so tender. I could not refuse to join with him to make a family."

The sisters left the room arm in arm and went out to the kitchen garden, where Beattie was pulling weeds. The elder looked up at her granddaughters and smiled to see that they were so happy. Though not a word, as yet, had been spoken between the three, she dropped her cultivator, walked quickly out through the garden gate, and said, "Hattie, I knew it! You are pregnant, aren't you?"

"Yes, Grammy. How did you know?"

"You look so radiant and pleased with yourself. Nothing else would make you look that way," she said as she pulled Hattie into a bear hug. "You waited, perhaps not as long as I wished, but you did delay both before and after marriage. You and Nathan respected my wishes. Now you will be sure to have a healthy baby."

22

Later that day, as the sisters sat in the sewing room, Hattie talked nonstop about all the good things that were happening in her life. Nathan had purchased two new heifers for the farm. His mother, Eunice, was very nice to her. And wasn't it wonderful how the grandparents were so excited about the baby coming in a few months? Lizzie smiled and acknowledged all the stories, yet her concentration was on a bolt of cloth with a pattern of lovely roses.

"Lizzie, you seem so content these days. Does the sewing make you happy?" asked Hattie.

"Oh yes, Hattie. This is something that I can do completely on my own. I am good at it. It is something that Marm used to do. She was the first teacher I had."

"You know, I can barely remember her. Even though I was already six when she went to heaven, so much of that life has been forgotten. One thing I remember is her reading to us in the kitchen near the stove. But then, I remember you doing the same for me. Perhaps it is you that I remember."

"It is not surprising that you would forget that life. You have been through some pretty difficult times since then. That time you were living in Bethel and found the captain swinging from the rafters in the barn... 'Twould be enough to make me forget things also."

Hattie sat in silence. "You know, Aunt Emy always told her friends and neighbors that he had been killed at sea in some kind of accident, even though they all knew the truth. She nearly even convinced me that I had not found him. When Grandy came to get me, auntie made me promise to keep the secret. Until her death, she was sending letters to me asking me never to tell a soul the truth."

"Sad, isn't it, that people don't want to accept life's truths," said Lizzie. "With all that has happened to me—Marm's illness and death, Father's dislike for me, for us both, really, the horrible way I was treated by him and that hussy Rose—I still believe that God has given me this life for a purpose."

"What purpose?"

"Well, I am mature for my years. I know fully how to take care of a family, how to help a man be happy and successful, and I have a skill, my sewing, that could get me through the worst of times. I may not be the most beautiful woman in the county, but I have very little more to learn to be a strong woman."

Hattie hesitated for a couple of minutes, sipping her coffee and watching the seamstress at work. The needle flew back and forth. A sturdy seam formed quickly between two large pieces of a gown bodice.

Liz continued, "Your happiness with Nathan inspires me,

gives me hope that I, too, will be able to find a man as good as he to love as my own husband. Is he as kind to you as he seems to be?"

"Well, Lizzie, from the time that he and I first met here in Westbrook, he has treated me with great respect. Even during the honeymoon, when I resisted his advances, he respected my wishes to wait. I feared that he might become like our father, demanding to be serviced by Marm as if they were animals. He's not like that at all. So tender and passionate in bed."

Liz pretended not to listen to her sister speak so intimately of their sex life. She did hope that, when her time came, Henry would also be gentle and tender, but in the several weeks before he left, as her intimacy with him had increased, he had been rough and had said some dirty things that bothered her. As a virgin, she was not sure what to expect, but she still looked forward to enjoying their sexual intimacies.

Hattie sat in silence for a few minutes as she became mesmerized by the movement of the sewing needle, which flew in a blur.

"What are you making? The fabric is so lovely," she said as she picked a scrap of cloth from the floor and felt the cool smoothness of linen.

"It is a wedding dress for a customer here in town. The cloth is finest Irish linen. Isn't the pink rose pattern lovely?"

Liz's smile caused Hattie to surmise that the dress might be for the maker, not the neighbor. However, she did not want to pry for news of a possible betrothal. Instead she switched to talk again about her own happy life. Liz paid little attention to the small talk, as she continued the work, smiling broadly all the time.

After a while, Hattie rose to bid farewell. "It is wonderful to see you so happy, Lizzie. Hopefully, whatever it is that pleases you will continue for the rest of your life. You deserve only the best of everything."

Rising from her work table, the seamstress threw her arms around her sister in such a passionate manner that Hattie was nearly knocked over. "Yes, I feel so free of past problems. The future is going to be to my liking, you can be sure of that!"

23

Henry Greene had always thought of himself as a realistic man, and he held no great illusions that the Whitcomb farm was going to be anything other than a run-down place. The letter he received from his friend Bert had explained that Abraham Whitcomb, in his eighties, was no longer able to keep up with things. His second wife, though ten years his junior, did not get around well due to a fall from a ladder in which she'd broken her hip.

However, when Henry arrived at the place on Mutiny Brook Road in what was known as West Waterford, he was pleasantly surprised. The small raised cape farmhouse was freshly painted. The barn was well maintained with its peak as straight as an arrow and the roof covered with newly installed shingles. A large hay field running uphill toward the rocky face of Beech Hill to the east had been recently mowed, and neat windrows of raked hay lay across the field. Beyond stood a proud grove of eighty-foot first-growth white pines. A small herd of Morgan horses, looking healthy and well groomed, were corralled behind the barn. There was even a small kitchen garden at one end of the house where pumpkins and winter squash lay ready for harvest.

Who had done all the work to make the farm so neat and pretty? Henry wondered. Not the farmer and his wife, that was certain. Perhaps a neighboring farmer was interested, like himself, in taking the place over. As he approached the house, his mind was in a bother. He would do anything to make sure that he had not come all this way for nothing.

He found Mrs. Whitcomb standing at the front door.

"I am Henry Greene. I've come over from Westbrook. My cousin Bert Learned told me your farm was for sale. I wrote your husband."

"Ah, yes. Abraham should be back any time. He just went to pick up some shook at Mr. Stanwood's bucket mill. He makes his own apple barrels, you know." She nearly shouted directly in his face. He would be surprised if the farmer was not hard of hearing.

'Yes. we have been expecting you," the woman continued. "As for the place being for sale, I can't speak to that. It is my husband's place, you know. Owned it before he even set eyes on me. Came down to him from his father, Abraham. Been in his family for three generations."

Henry excused himself, saying he wanted to rub down his horse. Could he tie it in the barn somewhere? She pointed to a stable door and bid him come back to wait by the fire. "The weather has turned so cold for late September."

In the stable, he found two other horses, both worn-out swaybacked mares, lying in dry hay. They looked so old, so tired from years of farm work. He led his sturdy American Quarter Horse to a vacant stall, removed the heavy saddle, and began to vigorously rub down the animal, which was sweaty from a long journey. Engrossed in the task as he was, he did not notice Abraham Whitcomb enter behind him. The farmer stood there watching for some time before he cleared his throat.

"Son, you're rubbing that animal so soundly that its skin might just come right off in your hand." His own words made the old man laugh so hard at himself that he coughed and then spit on the hay-covered floor.

Henry turned abruptly and, when he saw the old man coughing and smiling, he reached out to shake his hand. The farmer was a short man with a full beard wide enough to nearly cover his ears. He grabbed Henry's outstretched hand with a large calloused mitt so rough that it scratched Greene's hand.

"Mr. Whitcomb? I'm Henry Greene. I wrote—"

The farmer stopped him short. "Could be no one else would ride out here to the middle of nowhere. Been expectin' you."

The accent was thick and choppy. He swallowed half of his words so that he was very difficult to understand. Henry had often heard men speak like this when he was a child in North Waterford. Since he had been living and working in Westbrook, his ear had become accustomed to quicker, clearer urban voices.

City people often made fun of such farmers' accents, saying it was a backwoods and uneducated way of speaking. Henry tried to read Whitcomb's lips to understand the words better, but the heavy beard hid his mouth.

"Please put your horse up and come join me and my wife for a farm dinner. Won't be as fancy as what you might be used to, but it is good home cookin'. She may be lame, but she cooks real well."

24

Following a good country dinner of poached fowl, new potatoes, and carrots, Henry and Abe Whitcomb retired to the parlor to discuss business. They needed to get to know each other better, and both had many questions. They studied each other in silence as the old man lit his clay pipe with a stick he had stuck into a small cast-iron woodstove inserted in the fireplace. Whitcomb wore a pair of woolen breeches that had been patched so many times, it was hard to tell what the original color had been. These were held up with both a leather belt and a pair of black suspenders. No chance his pants would fall, thought Henry with a grin.

"You've got quite a nice lot of pasture spreading out to the mountain. Do you own all the way up to the bald face?"

"Used to, but I have been selling off pieces here and there to cover expenses. Sold that topmost lot to the Kimball brothers from North Waterford. They want to mine for mica up there. 'Bout all it's good for, really. That and the timber. That lot is virgin growth. Never been so much as thinned. Some of the pines are over a hundred feet tall."

"I would think it difficult to get the logs back down from the top," commented Henry.

"Nope. Just roll 'em down the hill in the winter. Or run 'em over the top into Mutiny Brook and collect 'em down near Bear Pond in the spring."

Henry could not tell if the man was kidding him or not. Everything was said with a straight face.

"Son, have you ever worked a woodlot?"

"No, but I have a brother who works in the woods each winter at a logging camp up Rangeley. He knows the work very well."

"Do you know farming? Haying? Now that's a skill that anyone can learn. Just have the right equipment. That's all. I have everything you need. It's included in the deed."

Henry didn't like the way this conversation was going. After all, he was offering to buy the place. He did not need to be interviewed about his experience. He didn't think he was applying for a job.

"Tell me, Sir, how is it that your buildings and fields are in such good condition? Do you have a hired man or a good neighbor helping you with the work?"

"Well, Henry, as old as I am and with the wife not gettin' around well anymore, you guess right that we have help. My daughter's two children are helpin' keep the farm in shape. The son, Ronnie, is good with mowing and machinery. He just finished storing the hay for winter. The daughter is excellent at gardening and hand work. Just restained the barn. She'll make someone a good little wife when she grows."

"Isn't the boy interested in having the farm himself?"

"I thought he might. Was willing to deed it right over to him. But he wants a formal education. Off to Bates next month. Wants to be a lawyer. You know, I had two sons who would have taken over, but both died at Antietam in sixty-two. It was so hard to lose both like that. We two have never been the same. My girl never had no interest in agriculture. Married a banker in Norway as soon as she was out of school. A fine man."

The old man stopped talking and sat in silence. He had lost energy for any further conversation this night. He rose from his seat and asked his leave for the night. Henry, who had been given a first-floor bedroom overlooking the mountain as his own for the night, was also tired. Before retiring, he stepped out onto the pasture verge and studied the land in pale moonlight. A western breeze was freshening and pushing towering cumulus clouds, still ablaze in sunlight, over the hilltop. Red and yellow foliage of tall maples, mixed in hedgerows with smaller and lighter hemlocks, was so full that the trees seemed to grab each breeze as would the sails of a ship. They swayed in gusts that probably marked the approach of a squall. He thought he heard a cardinal chip-chip-chipping in the distance. He was sure that he could make a pleasant home here for himself and his wife-to-be. He would run the farm at a profit. She would make his home life one of comfort and pleasure.

25

That night, a tremendous squall blew in from the north across Beech Hill. One clap of thunder woke Henry with a start. In the darkness of a strange room, he was disoriented, but then a series of lightning flashes lit up the single window so that he was able to go to it and peer out at an incredible scene. Never had he seen such a light show. Flash after flash lit the pasture, forest, and naked mountaintop as bright as day. He could make out tall pines high on the ridge, whipping in savage gusts as continuous spears of lightning danced through the clouds. Then came thunder claps in rapid succession, so loud he had to cover his ears at times. On and on the tumult went until one jagged bolt exploded into a massive oak just across the nearest pasture. The tree burst into flame, a gigantic torch against the dark sky.

Oddly, there was no rain with this storm, just light and noise. The flaming oak was so bright that Henry was able to make his way out of the room, across to the main door, and into the front yard. As he approached the pasture, to his shock and horror, he saw seven horses lying on the ground around the burning tree. He warily walked into the midst of a macabre scene of steaming horse flesh bathed in light from the burning tree trunk. With his bare foot, he nudged the legs of one horse after another. Clearly they were all dead, victims of that mighty bolt. He sensed that he had witnessed an act of Nature so cruel that he fell to his knees and prayed to God in heaven.

He stayed in that position for many minutes, lost in awe until loud voices brought him back to his senses. As the Whitcombs came running from the house, they moaned and wailed at the awful thing that had happened. With them, running from the barn, came a girl he had not seen before. She screamed when she realized what had occurred.

"No....No...No! Grandfather, our horses!" She fell to the ground as tears streamed down her face. Her hands beat upon the earth and pulled up tufts of grass. When she put her hands to her face to rub her eyes, grass and dirt mixed with her long hair.

Farmer Whitcomb rushed to the girl, lifted her up, and turned her away from the horses so that she would look into his eyes. He stared into her face, gently shaking her to stop the fit of grief.

"Aphia, it is an act of God. We cannot control what the Almighty does."

26

The four witnesses to this horror returned together to the house. Each in his own way sought solace through silent prayer. Abraham, Elizabeth, and Aphia held hands with bowed heads. Henry stood off to the side, alone in his thoughts. After a while, the farmer reached out to touch his guest's arm and pulled him into the circle.

"Henry, this is my granddaughter, Aphia, the one that I mentioned who does jobs for us around the place. She has been back home in school, but has a few days with us now. She has been grooming and caring for the horses as one of her main jobs. The loss hurts her deeply."

Henry had been watching the girl closely during the time they prayed. She was a beautiful young woman, one of the most beautiful he had ever seen, the type of woman he had always desired. Nearly as tall as he, she appeared to be eighteen or nineteen years of age, far past the age of public or common schools. Perhaps she was in a college or preparatory school. Her figure was stunning, her complexion clear and lovely despite puffiness brought on by crying. Muddy streaks marked her cheeks.

"Aphia, I am so sorry for your loss," said Henry. "These horses were such beautiful animals. Something this horrible must be devastating to you."

"Yes, sir. It is a tragedy." Words came hard to her. "For Grandpa Abe, this loss is much worse. He loved them as I did, and though he gives me credit, he groomed and cared for them much more than I. He also bought them and paid for their feed. It is a financial loss to him as well."

Her words impressed Henry as those of a woman who knew the value of things, understood the dollars and cents of life, as did Lizzie, but her beauty and luscious figure far outshone those of his fiancée.

He turned to the farmer and his wife, held hands with each for a moment, then released Elizabeth Whitcomb's hand long enough to reach out and take the girl's hand in his. They stood silently praying in a circle for a few moments. Then, without a word, they released their hands and returned to their rooms to privately contemplate all that they had just witnessed.

27

"So many bodies to get rid of," Abe lamented as he paced back and forth in the pasture inspecting the dead horses at dawn next morning. Only eight hours had passed, but the smell of rotting flesh spread across the entire farm on a freshening breeze. Swarms of flies buzzed around the worst burned areas on each carcass. "The smell of death is like to be here on this spot for years to come."

Aphia had been with him at first, but she was so overcome with grief that he sent her to her room. Elizabeth, too, was grief-stricken. Yet the need to rid themselves of such a ghastly presence drove her to anger. "Abe, you must do something! These flies are already in the kitchen. Soon the vultures will start to gather and pick the bodies apart. You have to take care of this!"

Abe knew of a slaughterhouse in Harrison that would surely

be pleased to render one or two of the horses into fat and leather. He himself might butcher one carcass for meat and tallow for candle making, but there were seven to be disposed of. When Henry appeared, he offered to ride to Harrison to find out if the butcher had any interest.

"Tell the man he can have these bodies at no charge—take as many as he wants," said Abe. "While you are gone I will start digging a big hole where we might lay these beauties to rest. What a damned curse!"

While Henry was gone, the old farmer began to dig a shallow grave along the base of a stone wall behind the burned tree. As he dug, it came to him that it might be better to burn the bodies in a large pit. It would be easier work, but a fire to dispose of this much horse flesh would burn for days and would use up a good portion of the driest firewood set aside for winter. Perhaps a combination of burning and burying would be the best solution. As he slowly continued to dig, Aphia approached with her own spade, and despite the tears that remained in her eyes, proceeded at a much faster pace than her grandfather. Soon they had made a shallow pit large enough to hold four bodies. They waited for Henry's return so that the three together might drag each horse to the pit. Abe brought a wheelbarrow of logs from the barn to start a very hot blaze that would, he hoped, reduce his prized animals to ashes.

Upon his return, Henry had mixed news. "The butcher will take two bodies, but unless you can deliver them, he won't be able to get here for a week or so."

"Damn, him!" shouted Abe. "We can't wait that long. They are festering as we stand here. Look, the bellies are beginning to swell already. We must burn them all and bury the ashes as soon as possible."

For two weeks, the fire burned, until what remained could be covered with soil and debris. As the final shovelfuls were smoothed on what had become a small hillock, smoke still carried the smell of putrid flesh up through the covering. Aphia, who had done so much of the work, turned to both men and said,

"This little rise in the land will always be a graveyard. Nothing will ever be planted here. It is a monument to death."

28

Aphia Stevens was quite tall for fourteen, and she had the looks and airs of a much older woman. Her public school friends were often jealous, resenting the attention given to her by boys her own age and even those who had graduated from high school. Several of Rosamond Stevens's good friends had actually stopped visiting with their husbands because the men flirted with the young girl. Exasperated by two incidents in which older boys had followed Aphia home from school and stood around in front of the house refusing to leave and shouting out for her daughter to come outside, Rosamond had taken to sending her to visit the Whitcomb farm for the summer and school holidays. Waterford, so rural compared to Norway, seemed to be a safe haven.

The girl took well to her home away from home, doing whatever household and farm chores needed to be done. Her grandmother, who was quite lame, was ever so grateful for the assistance with household chores. Aphia was especially fond of time spent with Grandpa Abe. She rushed to complete laundry, cleaning, and other indoor work each morning in order to help with haying, plowing, and caring for the Morgan horses that he was raising to sell.

She was also strong for such a young woman, nearly keeping up with older brother Ron when he mowed and gathered hay while off from school. Farmer Whitcomb sometimes chastised his granddaughter for "working like a boy," but he was most impressed with her stamina.

"Aphia, dear girl, when you are old enough to marry, it might prove hard to find a husband who wants a wife as strong as he is," he chided her in jest.

"Then, I'll not marry. I will just stay here with you and the horses."

She loved the farm life so much that, upon return to school

after each vacation, Aphia found it very difficult to concentrate on classwork. Her mind wandered back to Waterford when she was supposed to be studying. In particular, she obsessed over the horses, which now numbered nine: two old work nags that had been there many years and the seven prize Morgans. Her grandfather had purchased these over time, as he could afford it, in order to boost farm income. Morgans were a popular military breed, good at pulling wagons with heavy loads, and could be readily sold to farmers and stage drivers. During lectures, while other students diligently took notes, Aphia's pen would absent-mindedly sketch horse heads with a name scribbled under each. Her mother complained that she daydreamed most of the time, and though she completed most of the chores at home, her mind was usually elsewhere.

"Girl, you have got to concentrate on what you are supposed to be doing with your life," said her father one night after dinner.

She had just dropped her full dinner plate. Vegetables, chicken, and gravy lay scattered on the carpet. She cried out in frustration, hands waving around her head.

"Daddy, what is it I am supposed to be doing? My friends do not want to be with me anymore. Boys are always staring at me and making rude comments. I hate my teachers. I just want to go live with Grandpa on the farm."

"Aphia, you are an intelligent, hardworking young girl with a very bright life ahead of you. Farm life is not what you should be doing,"

On hands and knees, she picked up broken plate fragments and food from the floor, rushed to the kitchen, and tossed everything into a trash bucket. He did not know how she felt. He was just like Mom, always planning to ruin her life. Maybe she could run away, make believe she was eighteen, and get married. She looked old enough to perhaps marry a Waterford farmer who would buy the farm. Then she could be happy.

29

Henry Greene had lost all patience with the man. Over a month had passed since he arrived to purchase the farm and agreed to work to help the Whitcombs prepare for winter. He had made his financial situation very clear. He was ready to put $1000 down on the sale and follow up with mortgage payments if needed. Whitcomb had to know by now that he was capable of making a go of the family farm, and even do a better job than was now being done. It was time to finish the deal and make arrangements to contact Liz back in Westbrook. He approached Abe as the farmer was sharpening a scythe in the barn.

Henry began, "Sir, I have much appreciated you and your family's hospitality. We have worked together these past weeks to harvest the garden, repair a shed roof, and lime the pasture before winter. You and I have talked many times about my desire to own this farm and make improvements that you yourself have suggested.

"Each time I ask you to tell me what you want for the place, you change the subject. You either don't want to sell, or there is something about me that bothers you."

"No, no," the farmer stammered. "It is not you, son. I have seen that you are quite capable of doing the hard work needed to make a life here with a good helpmate. No. I have held back from reaching an agreement with you because there are two other considerations which I have been reluctant to bring up."

"Other considerations? Other than money?"

"Henry, I want little of your money. You are likely to need most of that for extras when you take over. Perhaps you might pay four hundred dollars to take care of me and the wife's expenses. What I need you to do in exchange for this farm I have lived on for over seventy years is this: first, we want you to agree to keep a room in the house, on the first floor, where the two of us may live until death. I will expect you to provide food for us, that is all, and we will pay you for it.

"Second, as I told you, my granddaughter Aphia loves the farm. She is a great strong worker and will make a good mother when her time comes. We want you to take her as your wife. She is young, yes, but she is so beautiful that, as she grows, she will bring light and joy to your days. If you do these two things, boy, my farm will be yours."

Henry's mouth hung agape. His breath stopped and his heart raced. These "other considerations" had never entered his mind.

"Abe, I need to think these things over, especially the second one. You know I have plans to bring a wife from Westbrook to join me here. How can I just drop her and marry Aphia? What of your daughter and her husband? What do they think of your plan? Abe, the girl is only fourteen, for God's sake!"

"Henry, there are always problems to work out with any plan. If you want this place, those are my needs. Think it over. We can speak of it again in the morning."

30

As weeks went by after Henry's departure for Waterford, Liz became concerned about the future he had promised her. Of course, she thought at first that he would soon return or send a letter to request that she join him. He did send a short letter early on explaining that the farmer had hired him to help close the place down for the winter. Yet as weeks went by, her confidence in him waned. She left off work on the wedding dress and, to get her mind off her anxiety, switched to making dresses that neighbors had ordered and for which they would pay.

Once again, Hattie returned for what were becoming more and more regular visits. Although the relationship with Nathan was going well and a first child was soon due, she sought her older sister's and grandmother's advice on periods of loneliness that periodically bothered her. The two sisters sat with Beattie at the end of the long kitchen table.

Beattie began. "Your mother had such dark periods when she was still a girl in school. Often she would return home from class, go to her room, and not come down for our evening meal. When these low periods first began, Hi and I would coax her downstairs, but she might only poke at the food and sit in silence until we let her leave the table."

"Beattie," asked Liz, "Marm often left us two girls alone for long periods. We would play with our dolls or books until we grew bored. At last she would appear and make light of her absence, saying that she was napping or had gone for a walk, when we knew that she had been sitting quietly on the stoop."

"Yes," said Hattie, "I have found myself sitting alone in our bedroom for hours at a time doing nothing. Nathan has asked me what I am doing. I make up stories because it is embarrassing to lose track of time like that… It doesn't happen much, yet it bothers me. I know it bothers him, also."

"My dear girls, your mother was a serious type of person who often took the problems of the world as her own concerns. I thought those times when she was alone came from concern for others. It was only after the marriage that I realized there was something wrong deep down in her soul. And Sewell brought with him a dark burden."

The three sat in silence for quite a while, until each rose and went about their separate business. Liz returned to the sewing room and Hattie dropped by to say goodbye. She watched Lizzie's skilled hands seam two pieces of cloth through a new sewing machine. Pattern paper on the back of each section crinkled softly as the needle ran back and forth through it. It was amazing how quickly this new contraption made the work go.

"Lizzie, look how fast you go. In only a few weeks, you have been able to master that machine. I would be afraid to sew my skin instead of the cloth. These modern devices scare me. I haven't even been able to learn how to cook well on our new Universal iron range without burning the food—and it's been nearly two months since we got it."

Intent on her work, Liz did not respond immediately. At last she stopped for a moment to rest her hands and stretch her cramped neck. "My dear sister, this Singer New Family is the latest thing. I traveled down to Portland six weeks ago to order one, but I was able to bring it home with me on the train in a crate. Grandy put it together for me in a snap. You should see how many machines the Singer Center has in stock. It won't be too long before every seamstress in the region has one like this or better."

"Were you able to finish that lovely rose dress for your customer? I would love to see how it came out with this new equipment. Do you still have it?"

Liz returned to the job at hand and seemed not to have heard the question. There passed several minutes of tense silence until she spoke at last. "No. The lady told me that she was not in a big hurry. If there were other jobs pressing, I should do those first. So I decided to put it off and complete dresses ordered by two of Beattie's friends."

"I am sometimes envious of your ability to create such beautiful clothes. Perhaps you will be able to make a living with your skills in the future. Such prospects would surely please me, if I had them."

Lost in work once again, Liz ignored the comment. The younger woman again tried to strike up a conversation. "Sweet sister, you seem to be so sad of late. Perhaps I am wrong, but it was my thought that the dress was being made for yourself. It did look to be your size."

Liz stopped again, reached across the small sewing table, grabbed Hattie's hand, and pulled it back to rest above her heart. "I can't keep a thing from you, can I? So much of our troubled lives has been shared. Sometimes it seems we even share our thoughts.

"Yes, the dress is for me. I will wear it at my wedding, when that day comes. It has taken Henry so long to acquire the farm that I don't know what to think. When I hear that all has gone well in Waterford and that we are to be wed, I can easily return to finishing my own gown. I am worried that he has changed his mind."

Hattie, seeing that Liz was on the edge of crying, switched the subject so as not to aggravate her sister even more. She had many questions to ask, but those were best left for a later time. She had, after all, come today with a special request for her sister.

"Could you do me a favor, Lizzie? Nathan and I have decided to move to a larger house before the baby arrives in June, and he has found a fabulous Victorian place in Bridgton. It sits up above Highland Lake on Main Street with views through many large windows down to the water. We have sixteen windows; can you believe so many? Would you have the time to make curtains for me? I can get the fabric in Portland, but the sewing is far beyond me."

"What wonderful news about the new house! I would love to visit you for a couple of days, take measurements, and spend time together. Perhaps we can find a bolt of fabric here in my closet that might fit your fancy. Let's look."

As they picked through her inventory of remnants, Lizzie's mind temporarily cleared of fearful thoughts about the future. They did not find a fabric suitable for the curtains, but they made a date to travel down to Portland together the following week to search for one in several of the fabric shops that sold to Liz regularly. Since Nathan often went to the city for business, he was sure to be able to drive them down.

31

The night after the farmer's final offer, Henry didn't even make an effort to sleep. All night he sat at the window or paced back and forth in his room, trying to figure out how to handle Abe's terms. Finally sitting down at a small table with a candle before him, he wrote down a list of good and bad things about choosing or rejecting the offer. This was a decision-making technique called the Ben Franklin, taught to him by his own father. Whether Franklin had invented it or not was of no concern to Henry, who had found it a good way out of past dilemmas.

First came the plusses of accepting the farmer's terms: ownership of the land, all of the equipment needed to run the farm, a beautiful young wife, a small investment, peaceful and beautiful surroundings, a valuable woodlot. Then he listed the minuses: abandoning Liz, negotiating with Aphia's parents, having to provide for the Whitcombs. Comparing the lists objectively, he saw that the good items outnumbered the bad. The choice was clear. He decided then and there to meet with Abe in the morning and do what must be done to close the deal. He was not going to miss out on this opportunity of a lifetime because of promises he had made in the past. Liz was a strong girl. She would be able to handle one more disappointment in her already troubled life. It was unfortunate, but not for him. He would have a wonderful spread of land and a very beautiful wife in the bargain.

Still, he was unable to sleep.

32

When the letter at last arrived for Liz, she was away visiting Hattie in the family's new Bridgton house. Gram came back from the post office with it and saw from the return address that it was, indeed, from Henry. It was all she could to do to keep from opening it.

I won't even tell the mister about it, she thought. He would be in torment for the next few days until Lizzie returns.

It went into a tea canister behind the chimney smoke box, a place he probably did not even know existed. He never spent that much time in and around the hearth except to light a fire on occasion.

Liz returned on Monday evening with several bolts of linen and measurements for sixteen windows. She was excited to relate to her grandparents how lovely the house was and how happy both her sister and brother-in-law were to have a grand townhouse in which to raise their growing family. Their family would soon include the baby and Nathan's ailing mother, who could no longer work on the farm and would move in with them. Nathan had taken a job as a salesman for a Cumberland County agricultural cooperative with an office in Bridgton. He might be away from home much of the time, but the salary he would receive would give them a much more comfortable life.

After a late dinner, Beattie went into the parlor, where Lizzie was cutting fabric for the curtains. She took the letter from her apron pocket and placed it on the work table. Liz peered at it, quickly halted work, and began to open the envelope. She hesitated for a moment, as if wanting to read her fiancé's words in private. Beattie excused herself to wash dishes.

As Liz began to read Henry's words, a smile came to her face as she considered how clear and neat his penmanship had become with her instruction.

Dear Liz,

Please accept my deepest apologies for the long delay in getting this letter to you. As I mentioned before, Farmer Whitcomb and his wife had hired me to do some work around this well-maintained farm. Farmer Whitcomb has been quite friendly, but also very reluctant to reach agreement on the sale. Negotiations have dragged on and on. He himself was born and has lived on the place his entire life and is reluctant to sell. However, we have reached agreement.

I pray that you and yours are healthy and happy. Did you get a chance to visit with your sister and Nathan?

As usual he was being very considerate. Such a dear, Liz thought, and read on:

After many conversations with the old farmer, we have at last reached an arrangement that makes it possible for the property to become mine for the small sum of $400. You can imagine how pleasing this is to me and how hopeful I am for a successful future here on this place.

Now she came to his explanation of the "considerations" terms. The smile left her face like the sun behind a storm cloud.

In order to reach a final agreement with Whitcomb, I have been forced to accept two unusual terms. First, I have agreed to provide a living place for the old couple until they die—a single room just off the kitchen—and to provide them food for which I will be paid. Apparently, here in Waterford this is a common consideration for sale of a family farm.

The second term is one which has given me great mental and moral turmoil. The farmer has a granddaughter who now lives with him much of the time, a wonderful young girl of fourteen years. In order for me to take ownership of the farm, I am required to marry this girl. Although such a consideration may not be as common as the first, it does happen occasionally. After much inner debate and consideration of the discussions you and I have had about the future, I have decided to wed the girl, Aphia.

Liz sat back on the chair with such a jerk that she nearly fell over backwards, the letter clutched in her hands. Her face flushed red first in anger, then in sadness, then in anger again. She could not finish reading and roughly shoved the letter into an apron pocket.

How dare he? she said to herself. What a crime he has done to me! What shall I do now? I am left with no future. He is just like my father!

Then, composing herself as much as possible in the situation, she rose from the chair, leaving all the sewing behind. She headed toward the door and silently passed Gram in the kitchen. The woman looked up from her chores, about to ask for a full report on the message, but Liz ran so fast toward her room that she was gone before the older woman could speak.

33

After several days of further discussion, a final purchase agreement was reached. Abe's wife and Aphia were then informed of what was going to happen. The old lady was pleased about securing a place to live until her death, but she was shocked by the second "consideration."

"Abraham Whitcomb, where in hell did you come up with

this cockeyed idea? The girl just ain't ready for an arranged marriage. And it's not for you to be doing the arranging. What of Rosamond? Don't she and Amos get to make these decisions?"

Abe stared at her in silence for the longest time. Then he stepped up to her and pushed her so hard down onto a chair that she almost fell to the floor. In shock, she started to cry.

"I am taking things into my own hands. I have made sure you are taken care of even after I'm gone. I would think you would be happy about that. Now, I am going to make sure someone in this family keeps a hand in this farm. Aphia is not happy at home, we both know that, and she loves it here. Rosamond had the chance to give the place to the boy. It would have cost them nothing. This is the only way now. Woman, go along with me on this or go back with your own people over in Oxford."

She made no answer, but rose slowly from the chair, wiping her eyes with a dish towel. There was no choice for her. He had made up his mind.

When Aphia, who was with them for the weekend, heard the plan, she rushed to her grandad and gave him a big hug. Tears also came to her eyes, but they were tears of happiness. To be able to live on the farm had been her prayer for so long, and now it was a dream come true.

"Grampa, what a great surprise!" She hugged him again. "You know this is where I want to be—where I will be happy."

34

Next morning, Henry, Aphia, and Abe set off for Norway on the farmer's hay wagon to explain the "other considerations" to the girl's parents. Henry had no idea what he would say to her parents, thinking that he would let the farmer, who had hatched the scheme, do most of the talking. After all, the girl's mother was Abe's daughter. Neither man had much to say during the trip, so the girl sat between the two on the bench and talked on and on about how wonderful it would be to live on the farm with her grandfather. She didn't seem to grasp the idea that she was about to become a complete stranger's wife.

When they reached the Stevens house on Pleasant Street, Rosamond met them at the door.

"Dad, what the devil brings you all the way from Waterford on such a clear autumn day? Is it something that couldn't wait until Amos and I pick Aphia up next week?"

Before Abe could answer, the girl blurted out, "Mommy, Grampa wants me to marry this man and move to the farm. This is Henry Greene. He is from Waterford like you."

Rosamond laughed at first, thinking that her young daughter was joking. Then, when neither man smiled or interrupted, she put her left hand to her mouth and attempted to pull her daughter away from them with her right hand.

"What does she mean, Dad? Is she making this up?"

"No, dear. I am selling my farm to this man. He is going to take care of Elizabeth and me until we die. We want Aphia to be with us, too. She loves the farm so and will be such a help to us."

The woman called to her husband, who came out and greeted the visitors with a big smile, reaching for the farmer's hand.

Rosamond said, "You'll not likely be wanting to shake hands with either of these men when you hear the ridiculous scheme they have cooked up!"

Henry, who up to this point had said not a word, reached out to shake the man's outstretched hand. "I am Henry Greene. Abe here has agreed to sell me his farm, but tells me that I must marry your daughter in order to close the deal. Having that place is important to me, so I have agreed to his conditions."

Amos drew his hand back and looked intently at his father-in-law. "There is no way in hell you are going to take our Aphia from us. She is ours to raise, not yours, Abe. You've always wanted your farm to stay in the family, even though no one has an interest. Is this how you plan to get your way—steal our daughter? I'll have you in court before you can blink. You will not get away with it!"

At her father's words, Aphia stepped back and grabbed both Abe's and Henry's hands in hers. "I have agreed with his conditions also. I am not happy here in Norway. I want to be on the farm and will get there one way or another. Daddy, you cannot stop me."

"Young lady," said Amos, "if you leave this house and marry this complete stranger who is so much older than you, your life will be ruined. You know nothing about being a wife. You are being impudent and selfish."

"You and Mommy do not know what is best for me. Grampa cares more for me than you do. I will learn what I need to know to be a good wife to this man."

Amos glared at her. "If you leave this home and return to that farm with this man, you will be forever dead to both me and your mother."

Abe took his granddaughter's hands and began to lead her from the house. He turned to his daughter and said, "If anyone else in the family had wanted to work my farm, I would have given of it freely. Aphia loves the place. It will be hers and her husband's."

35

In her room at the rear of the first floor, Liz threw herself on the four-poster and cried until the pillow was soaked through. Tears of both anger and fear flowed unchecked for hours. She cried for the abandonment. She cried for the shame of being so foolish as to believe Henry would marry her, such a plain woman. The grief was so deep that she even cried for the loss of her dear departed mother. All of the painful things that had happened in the past came alive once again.

What can I do now? she mourned. He was my hope for the future. May he die tonight and go to the devil! Take that girl he married with him! My future is now as hopeless as my past.

In the darkness of her grief, any light from the good parts of life shone not at all. She had no thoughts of her sister Hattie, her lifelong companion. Nothing of the loving home in which she had lived for ten years with Hiram and Beattie. It was as if life had come to an end.

Beattie knocked lightly at her door and softly spoke. "Lizzie dear, are you ill? Can I get a comfrey tea for you?"

"No, Gram. I will be fine. My time of the month has come early. It came over me so quick, while I was working."

Gram stood back from the door. She knew it was not Liz's time of the month. That had already passed more than a week ago. The news in the letter from Henry must have been upsetting, so she decided to leave her granddaughter alone. Muffled crying started up again as the worried older woman stepped away.

Eventually, Liz sat up on the edge of the bed and looked around her room. Arranged on the dresser, washstand, table, and chair were cherished mementos of earlier times mixed with colorful fabrics of current projects. At the head of the bed lay two rag dolls made by Marm many years ago and a patriotic red, white, and blue flag quilt, the only thing of value ever given to her by her father's mother. None of these objects made any impression. In such a state of darkness and grief, she sat numb to the world. No thoughts came to mind. Her body would not move. She just stared for the longest time into the darkening night. There was no use lighting a candle; darkness had control and it would not be broken by light that night.

After a while, she put her head on the pillow, closed her eyes, and pretended to sleep until dawn, still in a house dress and sewing apron.

She did not leave the room in the morning. She lay on the bed simply staring and sighing. Several times, Beattie came to the door with the offer of food and water, but was turned away. Hiram tried his best to bring her out. He knocked on the door. Upon hearing nothing inside, he lifted the latch and saw his granddaughter still lying on the bed, fully dressed.

"Lizzie, please come out and go for a walk with me. The day is so mild and sunny for this time of year. Not at all windy. Just the type of weather you like to be outside."

"Grandy, I am afraid I'd be no good company for you today. I am ailing with what seems like influenza. You best stay away from for your own good."

"Dear girl, sunlight would do you much good."

She said nothing more to him, just turned her blank gaze to the wall. As he left the room, he heard the click of the lock behind him.

36

On the second day, at first light, there came a soft tapping at the door. Hattie's voice whispered quietly, "Dearie, Grandy sent a man to my home last night. He told me that you were sorely distressed, that something bad had happened to you. I came back with him straightaway. May I come in to sit with you?"

There was a moment of silence before the key turned and the door opened. Liz was a sorry sight, standing in rumpled clothes that she had been wearing for two days, and her eyes were red and puffy. Her hair was a mess of tangles.

"Yes, Little Sister, please come in. You might help to bring some ease to my suffering."

Liz took the crumpled, tear-drenched letter from her pocket and handed it to her sister. They sat together on the bed in silence as Hattie read Henry's woeful words. She shared so much in Liz's grief that tears came to her own eyes.

Then she asked, "What will you do now, my love? Yes, he has failed you, made a rotten decision for which he is bound to suffer. You will get beyond this, like so many other things in our lives. Your future has to be brighter than your past."

Liz recognized the truth of that counsel. It was as if her own better self was speaking through Hattie. Once again, her dear sister was there to share another low point in life. They had risen together above those troubles of the past many times. How could she let Henry's desertion ruin her life? Was this experience worse than what had already befallen her? There were many years ahead in which good things might happen. With a small bit of bright hope coming into her heart, Liz stood from the bed. The two girls wrapped their arms around each other, rocking back and forth and crying in the passion of both grief and its release.

During the next few weeks, Liz worked very hard to rise above her misfortune. Throwing herself into stitchery and housework, on the surface she appeared to neighbors and customers to be pleased with life. Her immediate family had been told some details of the letter, but chose not to speak of it in her presence unless she brought it up. Hattie was a very frequent visitor. That, as much as anything, made the days go well for everyone. Brother-in-law Nathan Hallett also visited each weekend and took the sisters out for buggy rides around Highland Lake.

After a time, Lizzie left the seclusion of the boardinghouse, where she had returned to regular chores, and visited the Halletts at their new Bridgton home. The curtains were a great success. Pale yellow fabric chosen for the project enhanced sunlight entering the windows. Even Nathan was pleased—so pleased that he took the sisters out to dinner. Several days later, while Lizzie was still with her, Hattie gave birth to her daughter, Francena. All the negative feelings held within Lizzie's soul were set aside for a time. Not only would this darling baby girl be the joy of the parents, she might also bring some light and joy to her aunt's world.

Upon returning to Westbrook, Liz tried to throw herself into doing work around the house. She took on new orders for dresses from Beattie's friends that would keep her so busy there would not be time to be morose and dwell on her losses; but it became clear that a major change in life would be needed to allow her to move on. Nathan, who was often in town on business, became a regular visitor, as was Hattie after her recovery from childbirth.

Several months later, after Francena's christening at the Bridgton Congregational Church, the family had dinner at a nearby restaurant. Nathan told Liz that one of his clients, a dress shop owner in the town of Saco, was looking for skilled seamstresses to manufacture a line of women's outfits that were becoming popular in Boston and New York City. That night, Liz decided that the time had come to leave the nest and see if there were really any good things coming to her life. The mill towns of Saco and Biddeford were close enough for regular visits to Bridgton and Westbrook, yet far enough away to provide the separation from the past she so heartily desired.

37

There were many things to be taken care of before she left for Saco, and none was more important than a long-planned letter to Henry. Twice before, she had tried to compose an angry response to his cruelty. Sitting at her sewing table, she stared down at pages of tan stationery, pen in hand. An angry message had been welling up within her for days, yet every time the pen tip left its well, words would not come.

How can I forgive him? she thought. He has abandoned me, thrown me aside like an empty bobbin. But if I do not forgive, I fear this sadness will stay with me forever...

Finally, as words began to flow, her eyes filled with tears. They fell to the page and mixed with wet ink. He would know from the smudges how deep were her grief and rage.

Dear Henry,

Your actions have left me both angry and sad. Anger at the way I have been treated rises within me to the height of Bear Mountain near your new home. Yet sadness fills my heart each day to overflowing.

I ask God each night why He ever even allowed us to meet. If I had not known you as a wonderful man, I would not have come to the state I am in now. If He had kept you away from me, you would not today be hated by all who knew you here in Westbrook. Surely we are both cursed.

My sister has told me not to write you, but to leave you to wonder, as long as you live, what your decision has done to me. However, my conscience needs to be cleared of fears that I treat you in the same manner you treated me: that I leave you with dark questions to bother your sleep for the rest of your days. My plan is to make a happy life for myself and, perhaps, for another man with whom I may raise a family. It is what I wish for you and your young wife.

Only know that, though I forgive you, the hurt which you have caused will never leave me. Fare well, Lizzie

38

It took a lot of talking by Abe to convince Reverend Shaw to perform the wedding at Wesleyan Chapel on Mill Hill Road. Such arranged weddings were no longer as accepted in the community as they had been before the war. Although the pastor, in his nineties and a long-time acquaintance of Abe Whitcomb, was of the old school, the fact that Aphia's parents were not involved in the arrangement put him off.

"Abe," said Shaw, who sat in one of the church pews. "You are not her legal guardian. How can you deny your daughter's right to say who can or can't marry her daughter?"

"John, you know that here in town there are no regulations relating to adoption. My friend, I know that you have two children in your household right now that are not from your own family. They are not legally your offspring, but you treat them as if they are Shaws. My wife and I have adopted Aphia with her consent, of course. We will be living with her and Greene and keeping an eye out for her welfare. He is the owner of a large and well-kept farm and can take care of her. What more could a young wife want in life?"

The old minister, who needed two canes to walk, rose from the pew with much effort. "I will go along with this plan of yours if you promise to keep the wedding service small and do not invite a crowd. There are those here in town who would not look kindly on it. The fewer people who know about it, the better, as far as I am concerned."

Henry and Aphia's marriage, therefore, was a very, very small affair. Henry invited several cousins from the Willard family who still lived in South Waterford, but none accepted. Both of his parents were dead, and his sister, Matilda, had moved away to Massachusetts, never wishing to return to Maine. Aphia had only her grandparents in attendance. The rest of the family wanted nothing to do with the marriage. Amos had consulted with attorney Thomas Cook of Portland and had been advised that he was unlikely to be able to take any legal action because, despite the fact that his daughter was barely fifteen, the court would see her as old enough to consent to the marriage. Her new husband, who owned a working farm, would certainly be able to care for her safety and comfort, especially with close relatives Abe and Elizabeth living with them.

Only the day before the ceremony, as Elizabeth helped Aphia prepare an outfit for the occasion, did the girl begin to understand the significance of becoming the wife of a man she hardly knew.

"Elizabeth," she asked as the woman trimmed her auburn bangs, "I don't really like Henry. Most of the time he pays no attention to me. Once in a while, he is wanting to kiss me and hold my hand. When he sits next to me on the divan, he places his hand on my thigh. He is telling me that I have to start taking classes at the Grange on how to be a good housewife. That is not what I want to do. I'm just not going to marry him."

"I'm afraid it's a bit too late for that, Dearie," said the old lady. "If you want to live here with me and your Grampa, the wedding must go on. Don't you worry about liking the man; many women don't like the men they marry. You'll get used to him telling you what he wants you to do, and after a while, you'll figure out how to do just what you want. Maybe make him do your bidding instead of the other way around."

"Elizabeth, that is just not the way I want to live! My friends at school told me that a man might make me do horrible things in bed, things that don't seem normal. Henry has already started to grab my breasts and kiss me all over the neck like a sloppy dog. I don't know what to expect next, but I am sure it will not be to my liking."

"Aphia, didn't your mama talk to you about sex?"

"She told me it was something I would have to learn myself,

when I was married."

Elizabeth continued snipping at the girl's hair as she did her best to explain what her husband would expect of her. She felt it was important for Aphia to know at least the basics before the wedding night.

The service was set for Tuesday afternoon at a time when most people would be working in their fields or in the local mills that lined City Brook near the chapel. There was no procession, no music, no bouquet of colorful flowers to be thrown to waiting young friends. Aphia sadly parroted her vows and accepted the kiss given to her by a new husband, but her disdain for the man and her anxiety about the future, not happiness, made her cry.

39

As Liz was preparing to leave Westbrook for the prospect of a new life, her letter to Henry arrived at the South Waterford Post Office and was collected by Abraham Whitcomb on one of his regular visits to "The City," as the mill village was then known. William Watson, the Postmaster, had constructed the small post office building adjacent to his home with wood from his own sawmill on City Brook. His daughter, M'Etta Watson, worked at the office most days, and motioned to Abe as he entered the door.

"Your new man has a special delivery letter here from Westbrook. Do you want to take it to him?"

Whitcomb took the letter and studied the postmark and return address carefully. Knowing the story of Henry's former fiancée from stories told by the new owner of his farm, he was suspicious that this letter might mean trouble.

"Yes. Yes. I will make sure he gets it. Say, do you want me to sign for it in case it doesn't get where it's supposed to go?"

"No need, Abe. I know that Mr. Watson might ask for that. He's such a stickler with the regulations, you know—such a Republican."

They had a good laugh over the joke before Abe set out for the long walk home. Since the loss of his Morgans to the lightning strike, he had taken to walking a lot. It was a way for an old man to keep fit, and it allowed him to speak with neighbors in the big houses along Sweden Road. By the time he reached the farm on Blaguard Road, supper was nearly ready, so he put the letter in his pocket and sat with his wife and the newlyweds, Aphia and Henry, to dine. After dinner, he retired to his bedroom, having forgotten to deliver the letter.

The next morning, Henry was off to Oxford to attend a stock auction. He was to be gone all day, not planning to return until after dark, and by that time, the old man had forgotten completely about his duty to deliver the mail. That night, he went to bed and fell asleep, never to wake again. He had lived a good life of eighty-three years and was entitled to forget a few things at the end without worrying about St. Peter letting him through the Pearly Gates.

40

After a small funeral service at the Universalist Church and a graveside service at Elm Vale Cemetery on Sweden Road, Elizabeth Whitcomb and Aphia returned to the house while Henry attended a Grange meeting. The women began sorting out the dead man's belongings. The widow, rummaging through the pockets of his clothes, found a wrinkled, folded envelope with Henry's name on it. She passed it on to Aphia for safekeeping until Henry returned. The young girl stared at the handwriting and return address intently. She saw that it was from Liz in Westbrook, and knowing how upset the deserted woman might be, she decided to keep the letter from Henry. She felt that it was in his best interest, as well as her own, to hide it until such time as he and she knew each other better.

Not that the couple was unable to make a good marriage. On the contrary, they had been able to adapt to each other, after the fashion of the times, despite their lack of love for each other. He was teaching her all about her wifely duties, both those of the household and those of the bedroom. She was doing her best to learn cooking, sewing, and other domestic arts. She had also begun to enjoy some of their lovemaking, though he sometimes was a bit rough. It was just that there was such a difference in their interests. Henry wanted to farm and make money, raise a large family, and show off his beautiful young wife to everyone. She wanted to have friends her own age, and those whom she met in town were all unmarried. With these young girls she might go barefoot all day and go swimming whenever the weather was right. He kept telling her that she must grow up soon, take better care of the household, and learn to appreciate being an adult. Didn't she want a family? She was not sure.

After a few months, their differences became more defined, even divisive. This was not the man with whom Aphia wanted to have babies. When he tried to force himself on her, she would either succumb and regret it or push him away and run from the house. Before the year was out, she began to refuse his advances with harsh words and rebukes. He began to stay away more often, using various excuses such as looking at new equipment or stock for the farm, purchases that never arrived. As they grew apart, she was able to do more of what had been her original reason for being in Waterford: to work the farm and raise the new herd of Morgan colts that Abe had purchased just before his passing. Often, when Henry was at home, they found work to do that kept them apart, on differing schedules, so that even their meals went unshared. He reluctantly accepted this reality as the way their match was meant to be. She, who had never wanted the marriage in the first place, grew to dislike and eventually hate her husband.

41

Liz longed to stay and sort things out in the comfort of Westbrook, but her mind was set on the exciting journey to what would be a new world, where life would surely change for the better. It is difficult for anyone to leave a home where loved ones and friends always seem to step forward when you are in need. However, a clean new start seemed best after such a harrowing collapse in her dreams of happiness.

She would miss her grandparents and the busy boarding-house life. The thought of the two of them making do without her almost kept her from going. Hattie would not be there for her in times of both trouble and happiness. It was now going to be up to her alone to manufacture a new set of realities in the Saco/ Biddeford area. Yet her fondness for rural life made it difficult to leave. She relished the peace that she easily found simply walking in woods behind the house; she would miss the clean, cool well water and fresh produce from Beattie's garden. She was not exactly sure what to expect in the new environment, but she had heard from others who had worked in the mills and returned that it would be loud and hectic.

A large travel trunk was needed to carry her belongings on the journey, so Hiram pulled from the attic the one in which Francena's things had been stored since her funeral. He brought the chest to Lizzie, who emptied it, leaving what little remained of her mother's belongings on the bed. In this trunk there would be room for all that she wanted to take. There were clothes: an outfit for work and one for church, two pairs of new leather shoes, a lovely cotton shawl hand-knit by Grammy. She would take pairs of woolen socks, but also several pairs of silk stockings from a millinery in Portland just in case there might be parties, dates, or theater shows. Of course, she made sure there was room for her Singer sewing machine, though its weight made it impossible for her to carry the chest on her own. Also, there were books: a small Bible and several volumes that had belonged to her mother, ones that she had read so many times the pages were beginning to tear. Hattie loaned her a volume of Emerson's poems that she was sure were written during his visits to Waterford in the early years of the century. Liz had not opened it, but took it just in case there was time to read on the journey by coach to Portland and then on to Saco by rail. She had purchased two new novels she had planned on reading to the boarders in the evenings: *Huckleberry Finn* by Mark Twain and *Treasure Island* by Robert Louis Stevenson: Marm's beloved "R.L.S." These last were so recent that she doubted anyone she might meet would have read them.

In addition, one of the boarders, a grumpy old war veteran, had given her a thin yellow-jacketed novella called *The Saco Factory Girl*, one of the scandalous paperback books that had flourished over the past few years. It told the tale of a farm girl who loses her purity in a mill town and then her life in the sinful world of Manhattan. The man gave it to her with the following advice: "Girlie, you best be vigilant in that fast-paced world of lurid luxury. Beware of those Dandy Jacks with their fancy gold chains. You do not want to end up like Fitzallen's sorrowful heroine, lost to a life of sin and promiscuity on the streets of Spindle City."

Liz knew the man was well meaning, but after thumbing through several chapters, she knew that would not be her fate. She wasn't even going to the big city of Manhattan, just another small town in Maine. Still, the little volume might be perfect for travel reading.

She did not know what to do with Marm's old things that lay scattered on the bed. Perhaps Hattie would keep them in the attic of her new house. The clothes were sere and tattered, the quilt moth-eaten, yet somehow these relics needed to be preserved in memory of the dead. Liz put all these reminders into a neat pile, wrapped them in a remnant of colorful cloth, and stored them on the top shelf of her closet.

Just after breakfast the next morning, Hiram pulled his horse and buggy up to the front door. He offered to load the trunk, but couldn't heft it alone. One of the newer young workers, on his way to the quarry, grabbed hold of the chest, lifted it onto his back, and set it gently on the rear seat.

"Thank you kindly, sir" said Liz as she climbed to her seat. The handsome young man said nothing in return, just tipped his hat. She would miss the kindness and consideration of these folks, even the ones she didn't know.

They gave themselves plenty of extra time to travel to the Forest Avenue station at Morrill's Corner. The morning was warm and clear. Several times along the road, Hiram saw a friend and stopped to pass the time of day. Lizzie kept an eye on her pocket watch, but was enjoying the start of her new future. Over the three-hour journey, there was time for them to discuss the many changes coming to their lives.

"Grandy, I think your plan to sell the mine to Mr. Pride is a good one. You and Grammy have earned the right to be able to slow down and enjoy your time together. You have been working so hard for so many years."

"You know, Dearie, we could likely still make a go of the business, but Pride has made us a very reasonable offer. With his backers, he will be able to modernize the operation with pneumatic drills and newer equipment far beyond what I could afford. He is willing to keep my hand in the business for a time to train the newer men."

"Are you going to sell the house and move closer to town?"

"No; Bea wants to keep her garden. I like having the space around me. We will keep the place and some boarders, if possible. Rents will help on our expenses. Besides, if you ever decide to return to Westbrook, there will be a place for you."

"I certainly will come back for visits! But if I find the life I hope to find, I won't be moving back home to live anytime soon. With the wages they pay in Saco, I will be able to send a bit of money back to you to help out."

He smiled across at her as they approached the trolley platform. "Whatever you send back we will put in a bank account for you. If you do change your mind, that would be a nest egg for you to use in setting yourself up as a seamstress hereabouts."

That, she thought, was an idea worth tucking away for the future.

When the horse-drawn passenger car pulled up to the station, Hiram paid a young man to transfer her chest to the baggage compartment. Then, as he gave her a hand down from the buckboard, he pressed her hand to his lips. On the platform they embraced as she stepped onto the brightly painted trolley and found a seat just behind the driver. As the car departed, Liz realized that her world would never be the same again. This lovely old man in his gray homespun work suit would return to the slow world to which she was accustomed. The new modern world was to be her testing ground.

42

In the months following Abe's death, Elizabeth Whitcomb began to keep more to herself, often staying in her room for days at a time, only coming out for food when no one else was in the house. Her left leg, the one she had broken years ago, became very painful, making it nearly impossible to take care of the kitchen, the herb gardens, and the other household chores she had done for years.

One day she heard Aphia singing to herself in the kitchen and ventured out.

"Girl, you do sound happy today. What's the occasion?"

"Oh, nothing really. It is just that, when Henry is away, I feel a lot happier. He's not been here for over a week now."

"So sad," said the old lady. "When Abe would go away for a day or two, I would miss him somethin' horrible. He took care of so much here on the place, and I loved having him around."

"I can't say the same thing about my husband. In fact, if he stayed away for the rest of my life, that would please me the most. Even when he is around, we don't speak. He doesn't help take care of the horses. The fields need mowing, but he is not around to take care of that, either."

Saddened by her granddaughter's complaints, Elizabeth exited the house into the dooryard herb garden, which was overgrown with autumn weeds. When she bent down to pull a ragweed, her leg gave out and she fell into a woody lavender plant whose branches raked the thin skin of her upper arms. Aphia, hearing loud cries, rushed to the woman's side and pulled her up from the ground.

"What are you doing, woman?" asked the girl. "Are you all right? Look, you've cut yourself! There's blood on your dress!"

"Dear me! I've broken all the branches on the lavender! After all these years of taking such good care of my herbs, now I can't even pull a weed."

Back in the kitchen, the two sat across the maple gate-leg table Abe had made for his first wife. Aphia poured a cup of water for Elizabeth and wiped blood off the wounds.

"Grandma, would you like me to take care of those herbs for you? I would be glad to do it, but you must teach me how. I am sure that each plant must have different needs."

"Yes, you are right. And each herb has different uses, too. Some are for cooking, some for making and scenting soap. Some, such as that lovely old purple-flowered aconite or monkshood, have old medicinal uses. A little of that one can help to drive out a cold or soothe monthly cramps; but a large amount of the root might kill one of your horses. Even the flowers and leaves can poison you through your skin. Reach that little book over on the shelf—that one titled Culpepper's Herbal. It is one of my handbooks for the kitchen garden. You will see all my notes and the dog-eared pages for my favorites."

43

At the St. John Street station in Portland, Liz transferred from the horse drawn trolley to a three-car Boston and Maine train with a huge gray steam locomotive. The train was already nearly filled with travelers when she boarded. Some young women, who carried their clothes in canvas duffels, spoke to each other in French. Several young, well-dressed men, who also spoke the language of Canada, flirted with these girls. As Liz looked around for a place to sit, one of the men gave her his seat with a flourish and a bow. He stood in the aisle right up against her for a long time until a conductor approached and asked him to take a seat. A pair of old men sat in the rear seats smoking their pipes. Two women, perhaps their wives, sat just in front of them and knitted as they chatted. These four were dressed much the same as Grammy and Grandy. They were farmers, she guessed.

Departure was unlike anything she had ever experienced. Whistles screamed to clear the tracks. Large steel wheels screeched against the tracks as the train began to move. Through the several windows that were left open for ventilation, steam smelling like machine oil enveloped the passengers. Liz coughed and put a white handkerchief to her face. The yellow-jacketed novel she had chosen for the trip fell from her coat pocket. The man who had given her his seat picked it up, looked at the lurid cover, smiled broadly and handed it to her. She hoped that he did not think her immodest for reading such trash. He did try to strike up conversations several times along the way, but since she did not understand his language, he was easy to ignore.

Arriving at the Saco Island station on Main Street, Liz was overwhelmed with what she saw when the car door slid open. Passengers walked onto a crowded platform filled with uniformed porters, as well as hawkers of newspapers, jewelry, hats, cigarettes, and clothing for both ladies and gents. There was a cacophony of voices in confusing accents and languages she had never heard back home. On either side of the tracks, brick and granite buildings stood six or eight stories high. Horse-drawn carriages of all sorts moved swiftly in both directions on the main street, and in the distance she spied a brightly painted trolley with open sides being drawn by very large draft horses. As she watched, people were jumping on and off the car as it moved along the street. How strange she thought.

As soon as the luggage had been unloaded, a black-skinned porter hustled to her side with a small cart and said, "Lady, can I help you with that heavy trunk?"

He had a southern accent like one of the boarders back home who had come from Texas.

"Thank you, but I don't really know where you would take it right now. I don't have a place to stay."

"See those two ladies over there," he gestured to well-dressed women who carried signs with street addresses on them. "They can help you find a place to stay here in Milltown."

Liz approached the two while keeping a close eye on her trunk. Both women were dressed in fancy long dresses that nearly touched the dirty street. Both wore broad-brimmed hats held on with ribbons tied under their chins. The first one was deep in discussion with several other young female passengers. The second smiled at Liz and offered her hand and a business card with her name and the address of her rooming house.

"Are you looking for a nice place to live, dear? I have the cleanest accommodations in town. It's just behind Pepperell Square, near the Saco House Hotel."

"I am looking for a place that might be quiet, clean, and offer decent meals."

"We have a fine, clean kitchen. Can't say that it's real quiet, though." She smiled. " My dear, there really is no quiet place in town. Mills operate day and night now. There are always people on the street, no matter what the hour. My house is the best there is, and it is reasonable at one dollar and twenty-five cents per week, including breakfast and supper."

Liz agreed to inspect the place and gestured to the waiting porter to follow with her chest, which he loaded on his handcart. As the three stepped off the platform onto the street, a whistle screamed from one of the mill buildings. Her ears hurt. As she tried to cover them, her satchel dropped to the damp ground. The landlady grabbed it up quickly, threw it over her shoulder, and took her new tenant's hand.

"You are in a very different world now, girl."

44

This modern industrial world quickly shook the dirt of farm life off its new residents' boots. Everywhere Liz went, she met young women who were hurrying to adjust to the noise, a fast pace, and crowds of people far beyond anything they had experienced at home in order to earn wages many times better than anywhere else. Several thousand young men and women, many from Ireland, Canada, Greece, and England, as well as from small towns and villages around northern New England, worked long hours in the crowded conditions of the Pepperell and York Mill complexes where working conditions were crowded and sometimes dangerous. Banks of spinning and weaving machinery operating at high speeds might entrap a worker's limbs. Fiber-filled air had been known to ignite in flash fires under certain conditions, turning the work rooms into infernos.

Only twenty years had passed since an infamous disaster in a gigantic cotton mill in Lawrence, Massachusetts. On January 10, 1860, the Pemberton Mill, where nearly two hundred people worked, collapsed. More than a hundred souls, mostly women and children, were lost. The weight of machinery caused the second floor to collapse on the first, crushing all below. The building then burst into flame and burned for many days. This and other stories made Lizzie concerned with her own safety. Yet she was excited by this new and prosperous world.

With the letter of introduction provided by Nathan, Lizzie thought she might avoid such conditions. She expected to be working for a Mr. Donnell, an acquaintance and customer of her brother-in-law. She hoped that the small workshop in the rear of his dress shop on Main Street would be less like a big crowded factory where hundreds labored and that she might be able to use her sewing skills to create the latest in ladies' fashions. She approached the Donnell dress shop, but to her dismay, there was a large "CLOSED FOR REPAIRS" sign on the door. The windows were blocked with heavy paper, but she could hear the sounds of carpenters at work inside. It smelled as if a fire had recently burned in the rear, perhaps where the sewing took place. Disappointed, she turned away and headed off toward the Pepperell Mill complex.

I will find a temporary position there, she thought. When Mr. Donnell reopens, I go back and talk to him.

At the Pepperell, she sought out the main office, where a well-dressed overweight gent interviewed her for an entry-level job called "factory operative." This Mr. Webber was much older than several other men who appeared to be directing the work of many women her own age and a few young men. These men were dressed in shirts rolled up to their elbows, open waistcoats, and ties. Mr. Webber hired Liz on the spot because of her knowledge of fabric, gave her an employee badge, and asked her to return later that afternoon to work the second shift.

In exchange for six twelve-hour days of monotonous work, Liz, like other mill girls, received a wage of $5.25 per week. Such regular pay would make it possible for her to pay for room and board, as well as purchase little luxuries: jewelry and stylish clothes made locally to European designs. After covering the boardinghouse rent, she still might, if careful with expenses, have money to send back to Westbrook every month. Such financial freedom was a new experience, one that she and the other girls in her boardinghouse relished, given the limitations of their rural upbringings.

Liz felt much in common with two Irish sisters with whom she shared a room. Maeve and Mary Flaherty had left behind a broken home in a small town in western Ireland. During the potato famine years of the 1840s, their father had immigrated to America. When their mother passed on, their grandmother was left to raise them, just as had happened to Liz. Mary, the elder at twenty-five, had brought young Maeve to St. John, New Brunswick in Canada before crossing the border into Maine, promising to make a new life in America and to send money back to their family in County Clare each month. To cut expenses and allow for savings, the two women slept in the same bed. Since it was something they had done since childhood, it did not bother them, though the other residents found it odd. When Liz spent time with these girls, the manner in which they held onto and doted on each other reminded her of her own close relationship with Hattie.

Often on Sundays, the three women went together with others to the Opera House, where actors dressed in exotic Chinese costumes or as American Indians performed one-act dramas. Even though Sunday was the Lord's day, it was also the only day when the mills were closed. There might be church in the mornings, but the afternoons and evenings were times to enjoy.

One afternoon, the three women left the theater after attending a political drama about President Lincoln's assassination. As they strolled toward the boardinghouse after the show, Maeve noticed that a group of young factory boys who had been standing about, smoking and passing a bottle between themselves at the theater door, were walking close behind them.

"We be wantin' to keep an eye on those laddies" Maeve whispered.

"They look harmless to me," said Liz. She had not seen any of the young men before, but that was not unusual with so many people working and living in town.

"Harmless you say, but I'd not be trustin' 'em if I was alone right now." This time it was Mary who spoke. Her voice was a tense whisper.

The three linked arms as they walked toward home. Liz laughed as the Irish girls attempted to imitate some lines they recalled from the play. Out of the corner of her eye, she noticed that indeed, the six young men were catching up with them.

"Let's move a bit faster, girls. Those 'laddies' seem to be interested in us," said Liz.

Maeve turned abruptly, pointed her fist directly at the men and shouted loudly, "Get lost, you feckers! We don't like boys, if you get me drift."

So shocked were the stalkers that they stopped short and turned away.

"Maeve, you're quite the lady there with that language!" said Lizzie.

"The mother tongue I have. Brought it over with me from County Clare."

45

For three months, Lizzie labored diligently in the Pepperell Mill, working her way up from factory operative to "speeder tender," where she guided fast-moving strands of roving or raw fiber onto a machine that spun them into thread. The threads were then wound around spinning bobbins to be used in the weaving room downstairs. Her next position was to oversee a group of six women "tenders," as well as four young boys dubbed "bobbin doffers," who replaced full bobbins with empty ones. The men who operated the mill seemed to appreciate the diligence with which she worked. Further advancement might have been possible if she had stayed. However, the constant din of the machines and the monotonous twelve-hour shifts wore on her. She wanted to be able to design clothes and sew once more.

On her way home one night, she noticed that Donnell's store was again open for business, so the next day at her lunch break, she walked into the store and asked for the owner. To her surprise, the young man behind the counter was Mr. Donnell himself. He was very dapper in his white shirt, silk tie, and waistcoat.

"'Tis me you are looking for," he said with the slightest bit of brogue. "How can I help you?"

Passing him the introductory letter, she said, "Nathan Hallett has sent me to you to seek employment. I am Elizabeth Millet. I'm a seamstress."

"A seamstress, you say. Are you now? And what would you be wantin' to do for me? Clerk in my dress shop?"

"No. Sir. I wish to work in your back shop making the dresses and fashions that I see here in the store. Such a lovely collection of the latest styles. I know how to make those better than most girls."

He looked her carefully up and down. "I see by your outfit that you are a factory girl in one of the mills. The women who work for me in the back have come up a long way from the work that you are doing. I have no opening right now for a seamstress, but you might come in handy as a clerk. It doesn't pay as much, though more than what you're getting now, and the hours are more regular than what you have at present."

"Mr. Donnell, I will wait until you have an opening for a seamstress. Until that time, my current position is fine. Thank you for your time. I must return to work."

He gave her a critical look. She had just refused an opportunity to improve her situation, and that surprised him. Either she was a foolish girl or a smart one who knew what it was she wanted to do and was willing to wait.

As she exited the store, he shouted out to her. "Yes, miss, please check back with me in a week or so. There may be something open when one of my girls leaves to have her baby."

46

Another opportunity for advancement came very quickly after her visit to Donnell's. Mr. Moses Webber, the overseer of her spinning room and the man who had originally hired her, came to put a good deal of trust in her ability to follow his directions to the letter and to get the other girls to follow suit as well. He began to speak with her in a more personal way, very much the same as Grandy did. Such familiarity again reminded her of home and how much she missed the family.

One day Webber met her at shift change and politely spoke of how well she was working out at the mill. His manner was most kind and respectful, not like some of the younger supervisors who often used foul and abusive language to get the girls to work faster.

"Eliza, you seem a very capable young lady." He addressed her with a more refined version of her name. "You have a great ability to understand what it is that we at Pepperell are trying to do. We are becoming the largest exporter of cotton cloth to China, India, and Japan. Our ships are sailing up and down the east coast from Winter Harbor to Portsmouth, Boston, and New York. Rail is carrying our goods deep into the heart of the nation. It is workers like you that help us reach our goals."

"Sir, you are very kind to say that. I am pleased that you notice my work here. As a seamstress at home in Westbrook, the value of high-quality cloth was most important to me. I do my best to make sure our line does its job well."

He was surprised that she was a seamstress.

"Did you work by hand, or did you use a machine for your sewing?"

"Mr. Webber, I have a new Singer machine here in my room, but there never seems to be enough time in a day to use it. However, I do get to repair clothes for girls in the boardinghouse now and then."

From that day on, he started to bring fashion cards to her on which were color drawings of the latest outfits for men, women, and children like those that were becoming so popular in the clothing shops along Main Street and in big city markets. The styles were very much influenced by foreign designers, and the immigrant workers appreciated the European motifs. Liz had seen a few of the dress designs in the shops that she visited, Donnell's and Hamilton's. Men's styles in jackets, waistcoats, and shirts were so different from what the men at home wore. She had many questions about each card.

Webber himself had a small shop catering to men and boys. A horse-drawn wagon with a sign on it saying *WEBBER CLOTHING AND SHOE COMPANY. MEN'S AND BOYS. TOP TO TOE OUTFITTERS* was often seen making deliveries. In true Yankee fashion, it turned out, he also ran several small sewing rooms in the area behind City Hall, where seamstresses used Pepperell cloth to produce imitations of the latest imports.

Soon Liz was working in one of his rooms. She did not have to use her own treadle machine. Only the latest machinery, run by electricity, was used. The place was set up like a small model of the larger factory, but with better working conditions and much, much better pay. She earned $8.50 per week. That was sufficient to allow her to buy almost everything she wanted and still send money home each month. This was the life she had wanted to live. Still, each month when she posted a letter containing money to Westbrook, the urge to return home continued to be strong.

Several letters from home, one from Beattie and one from Hattie, had informed her of her sister's very difficult childbirth. Both mother and baby were fine, but the delivery had lasted nearly two days and had been followed by an infection that caused damage to the uterus and might make future pregnancies very stressful or not possible at all. Her concern distracted her from throwing herself completely into the new job, and she wrote to Hattie and offered to return to lend a hand.

Several days later, Nathan showed up at Webber's shop and invited her to dine with him at the Hotel Saco. He had been at home for the birth of his new daughter, but now was in Saco to meet with partners at the mill to discuss working for them to sell their fabrics in Boston and points south. As they headed toward the hotel, Nathan began to explain his exciting new venture to her. She wanted to hear how hard his wife's delivery had been.

"Nathan, I feel that I have sorely neglected her in a time of need. That is when we have always been so helpful to each other."

"No, Lizzie, there really was little that you could have done to make it any easier. During much of the time she was in labor, I myself was denied admittance to her room. Like me, you would have likely been relegated to sitting outside the door listening to her moaning. Even Beattie herself was unable to witness the ordeal for more than a few moments. And your grandfather was a terror, hollering at the birthers one minute and morosely staring into the fireplace for long periods. Life in the house ground to a halt."

"Is Hattie fully recovered now? It has been several weeks."

"She wanted me to assure you that she was on the road to complete recovery and would be ready for a good time with you over the holidays."

As their dinners arrived, he reached across the table and touched her forearm lightly for a moment. "I also wanted to share news with you from Waterford, if you will not be overly bothered. I have just returned from there."

"Please, Nathan, if this is news of Henry, please keep it to yourself. That man has done enough to ruin my life. I care not what he has been doing or if he is still even in this world."

He looked away, sorry that he had broached such a sore subject. She hardly touched her dinner and had very little else to say for the rest of the meal.

"I am sorry, Lizzie, for ruining the occasion. Trust me, I will never bring up the name of that bastard again in your presence."

47

Liz had been away for nearly ten months. She sorely missed her family and friends back in Westbrook, and as soon as Mr. Webber closed his sewing operation for the Christmas holidays, she was on the train back to Portland, where she caught a horse-drawn stage. Grandy met her at the new Westbrook station in an old chaise drawn by a handsome Morgan. It wasn't the most elegant mode of transport for a successful young lady, but it suited her just fine because she was home.

She wore a lovely European-style outfit made from the finest Pepperell cotton, which clearly set her apart from the homespun clothes still worn by most of the train passengers. Her hair was now bobbed in the current style with curls that just showed themselves around the edge of a pretty blue pillbox hat. Hiram still wore the rough pants and wool jacket that marked the working man. It was a far cry from the frock coats, vests, and white shirts she had been making at Webber's.

Arriving at the big white house on Pride's Corner, she wanted to jump from the wagon and run to see Beattie, but she waited for Grandy to offer her a hand down. It was the old manly way of helping a woman from a wagon. She had to let him know that she still respected his ways, even though that style of living was much slower than what she had been living in Saco.

"Thanks for the ride and for helping me down," she said.

"Bet you don't get much good manners from the boys down in Saco. Since all the young boys came back from the war, nobody seems to have time to act kindly."

Although 25 years had passed since General Grant's treaty was accepted by Lee at Appomattox Court House, Hiram and many of his age still looked back to the time before the war, when life seemed to be more gracious. His thinking, no matter how dated, was correct. She had found very few men in "Spindle City" who were respectful of women in the old manner.

"Grandy, times change rapidly in Saco. When I first went there last year, most factory workers were women my age or younger. Many of them were foreigners, some who couldn't speak English. Most of the men at the factory were managers or overseers. Often one would seek to take advantage of a woman, especially a younger foreign girl. Most of the managers, though, were moral men. No one ever tried anything with me."

"You do have a strong way about you, Lizzie...always have. They'd not dare to bother you."

She received his comment with a smile. "Recently many more young boys have come to the mills. They are better able to do the heavy work that keeps the machines going. Some have replaced women in the spinning and weaving rooms. You are correct that these lads, although they never went to war, don't seem to have the same values as I did growing up. They rush around everywhere, put great pride in the things they own, and seem to have lost a great deal of respect for us ladies."

During her time away, Liz had kept her distance from men who sought her favors. Memory of the hurt Henry had caused her still smoldered. Perhaps she might meet a faithful lover at some point, but it would likely be a man who, like herself, still lived by a rural set of standards. The fast-paced, tumultuous, modern lifestyle was not completely to her liking, though the financial rewards were most welcome.

"Beattie has cooked your favorite meal for your return. Hattie, Nathan, and the little one are in from Bridgton. Should be a gay old time tonight," said Hiram.

After he climbed back up on the wagon to get her bags, he peered back down at her. She noticed that even though he had aged some in the past months, he still stood proudly with a straight posture. His wide-brimmed hat was bent and a bit stained, but he remained the handsome man who had rescued her from Rose Millett's cruelty more than fifteen years before. He would always be a favorite, if only for that.

As Liz walked toward the house from the stable, Beattie opened the door. She stood with her arms open wide. A towel dangled from the top of her apron. As usual, since she had been cooking, she wore a baker's hairnet, yet her long gray hair hung down to her shoulders. Lizzie was glad that it had grown so long. It made her seem so much younger than her nearly seventy years.

"Lizzie! Lizzie! Come here quick! Give your old Beattie a hug and a kiss. So many times I have read and reread your letters these past few months. You have been away so long this time. Don't you look so much like your mother now, God bless her soul."

48

The first three days of her visit were a blur of constant activity. Hattie, Nathan, and baby Francena visited until the day after Christmas. Liz gave lovely gifts to the family, things she had made after work hours at Webber's. There was a beautiful shawl for Beattie, another of a different color for Hattie, a silk tie for Nathan, and a new white shirt for Hiram. She even had made a little plaid smock for her young niece. Everyone was pleased and surprised, especially Hiram. He sat speechless for a few moments, staring at the pure white cotton. It was something he had seen only in the magazines Beattie brought home once in a while.

Then he turned to her with a grin ear to ear. "Friends hereabouts will think me a real grandee with this shirt. No one I know of has anything to wear that is so clean and pure. Best be saved for church."

He smiled again as he rubbed the smooth cloth between his calloused fingers. "Lizzie, you are so talented, so skilled."

Later in the day, after supper, she sat alone with Hattie. Though they had kept in touch with occasional letters, they had not seen each other since the days before Liz had left. Hattie had tried to get away, but the combination of the work being done on the new house, a difficult birth, and raising her daughter had kept her very busy. The sisters had much catching up to do.

"Hattie, I was so worried about you when you wrote to tell me how ill you were after having the baby. Perhaps I should have come to Bridgton to see for myself how you were doing."

"No, no, Lizzie. It would not really have helped matters any. There was little to do but lie still and wait for the infection to go away. Dr. James told me just to stay put and drink lots of water to flush the infection out of my system. Yes, it would have been wonderful to see you, but things were not so important as to draw you away from that new job you have at Webber's. Tell me all about it."

"Well, it is just the job I was looking for. Mr. Webber is so kind to me. He puts his trust in me to make the most challenging new designs. There are four other women in the shop, but they are not as skilled as I."

"I am so happy for you, Liz. You have always had a great talent and now you are getting your chance to shine. Sometimes I wish I had that kind of talent. To make your way successfully on your own terms must be wonderful."

"Yes, it is, but you are also successful on your own terms. You have a wonderful husband who adores and respects you and now a healthy daughter. I have always wanted a family of my own, but so far, that has been beyond my reach. At twenty-five years, I still have time to follow your example."

"Sister dear, be in no hurry to follow in my footsteps. The sad periods of loneliness which you know I have suffered in the past have recently become more regular. Nathan urges me to see a doctor or perhaps take the water cure, as it may be some form of mental illness or melancholia. If these are part and parcel of the life I lead, you might be wise to stay on your own course."

Lizzie grabbed both of her sister's hands and kissed the open palm of each. "We both continue to carry the burdens of the past in our hearts and minds. These are illnesses that may linger in our blood. Let's pray that we figure out how to break the mold."

"You, Liz, seem so happy and confident now. This new life agrees with you heartily. Surely you have made a new mold."

49

All during her holiday stay, she continued to share stories of her many experiences over the past few months and her pride in how successful she had become. Neighbors dropped by one after the other to welcome her back. She even went to church on Sunday with her grandparents, something she had not done for a long time. Seeing her grandfather in his new shirt was the main reason she went.

At last, when there was time after church to withdraw from the hubbub and consider what she might do next, she went once again to her room. She sat on the feather bed and looked around at changes made during her absence. Beattie had hooked a blue-and-gray rug for the floor. There was a new full-length mirror on the back of the closet door. A framed sketch of Hattie stood atop the washstand next to a big white china ewer. How wonderful to have such privacy after sharing a room with two others for so many months. While the time away had been rewarding and exciting, the rush of city life and absence from family continued to bother her. Country living, despite its slowness and occasional isolation, was more to her liking, though the money earned working for Webber's shop could never be made in Westbrook.

Beattie and Hiram had made it clear to her once again that if she decided to return to Westbrook and live with them, they would deed the big house over to her. The two of them were now going to keep a couple of rooms on the first floor as their home until they died, but the work of keeping such a place going had become too much. This proposal, as well as the nice little nest egg building up in Norway Savings Bank from the monthly sums she had sent home, made the idea of returning even more tempting.

The night before her scheduled return to Saco, a blizzard blasted into town, blanketing the village and surrounding areas under a foot and a half of snow. Drifts climbed to block the windows on the east side of the house. Travel was impossible. The delay gave her time to seriously consider her options. The snow was so beautiful, and after the storm, illumination from the moon lit the landscape like a Christmas card. Usually busy Forest Avenue was as still as a church during prayer. In Saco, snow was never really white, but rather gray. It seemed to turn brown as soon as it hit the earth. In the months of her absence, she had not experienced such peace, quiet, and natural beauty.

When, after two days, the roads were rolled and passable, Liz made the decision that it was still too soon to move back home. Memories of the agony caused by Henry's desertion and letter had often come to her in the long hours of work in Saco. Not the sadness of it; no, that had transformed with time into a symbol of a major turning point from a life of travails and struggles to a brighter life where she could control her fate and succeed at whatever she wanted to do. Yet that hurt still remained deep in her heart. More time and insight were needed before she could be free to return to the world where it had happened.

One of Hiram's young masons offered Liz a ride to the trolley station on his way to visit family in Gorham. Before leaving, she sat with both grandparents over an early breakfast of coffee and fresh-baked cornbread.

"I will miss my family once again," she began, "but I want just a bit more time to find myself. You two have been so kind to me for so many years. Your offer of the house and land is gracious beyond words, but I must delay in accepting it until my plans for the future are clearer."

"Lizzie girl," said Beattie, "Hiram and I want only the best for you. We want you to have a happy life from here on in. Lord knows, there has been enough unhappiness so far. We will make out very well here, even though you will be away. The two boarders that we kept on have worked out well. They seem to be willing to care for their own needs and help us with the chores."

"Yes, Liz, with sale of the quarry due to pass next month, you needn't worry about us. There will be plenty of money to cover our expenses. Just know that you are welcome here at any time. Our offer to you stands as long as we do," said Hiram.

Liz leaned across the table, grabbed and held hands with

them for a moment. "Please, please, please, know that I love you dearly. When I return for good you will see that I am ready to make a life together here with you."

Will Cain, her driver to the new station in Westbrook, entered the room as the three parted. She recognized him as the strong young man who had loaded the chest for her when she first traveled to Saco. He grabbed her satchel from the floor and went out to the buckboard. After waiting patiently for his passenger, he gave her a hand up to the seat before climbing up himself. She had noticed that he was shy, so the silence between them as he drove on was no surprise. She had not spent enough time with him to realize that the young man, perhaps three or four years her junior, was so handsome.

Finally, when they were about to reach the station, he spoke to her very slowly, as if considering each word before he said it.

"Ma'am, it must be a different living down there in Milltown. My sister was there at the mills for a year or so. She didn't much care for it. Too loud. Too fast. I have been there a couple of times to visit my uncle on his farm in Biddeford. The city's not the type of place for me."

"Will, it's just not for everyone, I guess. I'm lucky to be working in a small dress shop instead of a mill line. My first job was on the line, but I was glad to get a job outside the factory after a short time. I know the life of a mill girl can be tough."

"And dangerous!" he said loudly. "She lost a finger in an accident. Couldn't wait to get back home."

"Sorry to hear that. How is she now?"

"Oh, fine. She got married right after getting back. Seems happy."

When they arrived at the stop, Will helped her down and carried her bag to the platform. As he turned to go, she thanked him for the ride.

"Ma'am, please be careful down there. Don't want to see you get hurt or anything."

50

Back in Saco, Liz quickly settled back into her other life. Mary and Maeve were still her roommates, and she continued to work for Mr. Webber. Somehow, though, things felt a little different from when she had left because she now had a plan in her mind, a program and goals that had been missing before the Christmas break. She knew that she had changed, but as yet could not really explain the difference to her friends.

Webber himself continued to be impressed with her production. The speed and skill with which she designed and made clothing for both men and women was outstanding. He began to give newer designs to her rather than to the four other women who had worked in the shop for a longer time. One day he took her aside in his office with an exciting proposition.

"Elizabeth, you are very skilled. And you seem to get better with each design I give you. No one who has ever worked here has been able to study a dress from a fashion card and turn it out so quickly and so well."

"Sir, this is the work that I have always wanted to do. Each time you give me a new project, it seems that I understand more about the way the cloth pieces are meant to fit together."

"Dear, I have been thinking about a new job for you, one that could put this shop far ahead of the others in town. Everyone is copying the European styles that are selling in Boston and New York. I think that we might up the ante, so to speak, by having you actually design new styles that nobody has seen… Not that they would be totally different because we need to be competitive. The fashions would be American style, not foreign. The colors might be more muted, like homespun, but made, instead, with the mill's best-quality cloth."

She looked closely at him, trying to understand what he was saying. Would such a plan have merit? Could she do such a thing? The simple clothing styles that folks wore back home had lingering appeal to her, but she had come to appreciate the use of finer material in more modern designs. She thought that the clothes she made for herself might be prototypes for the style he was suggesting.

"Mr. Webber, I'm your girl. How do you propose we do this?"

"Dear, that is up to you. You know your strengths. I will listen to your suggestions and see if they make sense. It is important that we do this now, while winter has slowed business. When spring arrives, we must have new lines out and ready to impress.

"I will pay you well for this, Elizabeth. Your rate will now be twelve-fifty per week with an option to twenty dollars when things work out."

Her heart fluttered and her breath quickened. She had never heard of anyone making $20 a week. Now she could increase the money sent back to Westbrook, and that nest egg would grow much more quickly.

51

During the winter and early spring at her Beech Hill farm, Aphia was called upon to spend more and more time caring for Elizabeth Whitcomb, who was now nearly an invalid. Winter had been rough on both women, and the elder had been forced to take to her bed just after Christmas and had been there every day since. She could no longer walk. Her breathing had become seriously labored. She slept much of the time. The young woman continued to care for the five Morgans, which were housed in the barn during the worst of the cold season, but all of the household work, formerly shared, now fell upon her shoulders.

Henry was of little help. He was away much of the time visiting friends over in North Waterford. Even when at home, he took little part in sharing chores. He kept to himself as much as possible. Although the two might sit together at mealtime and sleep in the same bed most nights when he was home, he had stopped asking for her favors or forcing himself on her.

For the first time in her life, Aphia took on the added responsibilities in a very adult manner, sometimes resentful of the load she bore, but never complaining. Occasionally, when the need arose to do something that she had not done before, such as sewing to repair their clothes, baking a ham, or thawing the water pump, she would become an attentive student to her ailing grandmother.

"My dear girl, you have made my miserable existence a little easier this winter. God knows, you might have left me to suffer on my own and gone off with your friends from town more often. There's nary a thing to be done in the house that you don't now know how to do."

"You are so kind to say that, Granny. You have made it easy for me to learn how to be self-sufficient. With Grampa Abraham, before he died, you filled the larder with food to get us through. You know how to do so many things. As spring approaches, I will want to learn all about your gardens, so I can help to stock up for next year."

Once again Elizabeth wanted to teach the girl more about her herbs. Forgetting that they had begun the training months before, she said, "Aphia, over there on my dresser is a book by a Dr. Culpepper: his herbal. If you bring it to me, I can point out the plants which we have in the dooryard garden. It will soon be time to start the early season work. That garden has been my pride and joy since the day I came to live with Abe after his first wife passed. It was she who made the plant selections and left that book here in the kitchen Hoosier."

Although Aphia had already read the book from cover to cover after their first conversation, she brought it to Elizabeth. There was a long sheet of paper in the rear of the herbal. It listed all the plants in her herb garden, from aconite to wormwood. The two women reviewed each plant, discussing the best procedures for growing, harvesting, and using each. Elizabeth was very careful to touch upon the dangers of using too much of any plant that might be considered dangerous.

"While every part of the aconite or monkshood plant is poisonous if overapplied, Culpepper says it can also be a powerful healer." She read:

Whether we are made susceptible by a cold wind, stress, a shocking situation, fear or emotional strain, aconite specializes in helping our bodies cut short the diverse effects. These range from sudden cold, fever, or even hay fever symptoms including sniffles, sneezes, dry sore throat, dry cough and eye irritation; restlessness, anxiousness, and occasional sleeplessness; heavy headaches with a burning sensation, minor ear pain, teething pain; vomiting with sweating, strong thirst and a burning sensation in the stomach; and minor urinary irritation. Best taken as soon as possible at the initial phase of illness!

"I have used it many times to cure winter illnesses in both Abe and myself, but whereas one dram might cure a cold or ease a headache, two drams would bring nearly instant death. Even the beautiful purple flowers of the plant can be toxic. It is best to wear gloves when touching it."

52

Liz made little change in the way she lived, even with such an increase in pay. Room and board arrangements were the same. There may have been a few little fashion accessories added to the wardrobe occasionally, but nothing too showy. She found a tourmaline ring that went well with her gray eyes. The stone came from a quarry near Waterford, so she had to have it. The Irish girls were informed about her new job, but she did not reveal how much she earned.

One Sunday in early June, she treated them to a horse-drawn trolley ride across the bridge to Biddeford. In a barn on a farm just outside of town, a farmer was displaying a work of art that was the talk of the area. It was a painted mural called The Moving Panorama of Pilgrim's Progress, the work of a group of American artists including the great landscape painter Frederic Church.

When they approached the red barn, it was bustling with activity. Groups of men, women, and families wandered in and out of the building. A barker stood in a booth selling admission tickets for a nickel. Luther Bryant, who owned the place, had arranged to have a colorful printed brochure available, for sale as a souvenir, which told the story of how this "American masterpiece" had been touring the country since 1848 and had nearly been lost during the Civil War.

The three ladies entered a large open stable where a crowd shuffled about in the center of a canvas mural draped from the rafters to form a circular enclosure. On it were painted a series of vignettes depicting the adventures of a religious pilgrim named Christian as he sought redemption and eternal life. The images were life-size. Breezes moving through the barn made the canvas move, making figures of men, demons, giants, and damsels seem almost lifelike. The panorama was unlike anything ever seen in the area, and it left the women speechless as soon as they entered.

The two sisters wandered away, leaving Liz to her own reverie. Suddenly, from across the space, she heard her name spoken almost in a whisper.

"Ma'am. Miss Lizzie."

It was Will Cain. He was dressed in a homespun wool suit and wore a brown fedora. It took several minutes for her to recognize him.

"Will, what a surprise. This is the last place on earth I would have expected to see you."

"Yes, miss, it is a surprise for me as well. My Uncle Luther owns this barn. He invited me down to help him hang the murals. Personally, I can't make hide nor hair of the thing. Maybe that's because I'm not too religious."

"Oh…neither am I." She walked across to him. "But I love the allegory of it. If you have the time, walk with me around the circle and I will explain what is happening."

She took his arm in hers. He held back nervously at first, but as he relaxed and let her lead him about, she began to tell the story of Bunyan's Pilgrim's Progress.

"Please, Will, call me Liz."

When Maeve and Mary returned with programs, they hesitated to approach Liz, who was walking arm and arm with a tall, handsome, well-dressed young man. Deep in discussion, the couple seemed oblivious to the rest of the crowd.

"Mare," said Maeve to her sister, "perhaps we underestimated the wiles of dear Lizzie. She has her hooks in that young lad, leads him around like a heifer on a tether, she does."

"Nay. Nay…not a cow, dear one. She has drawn him in like a spider catches a fly."

Both laughed so loud at that comment that their friend saw them. She waved them to come over.

"Mary, Maeve, this is Will Cain. He works for my grandfather back in Westbrook at Pride's Quarry. His uncle is the man who owns this barn and has put the exhibition together."

"Oh, praise be to your uncle for doing this!" said Mary. "Tell him we love it. Reminds me of home, it does—so religious, like mass on Sunday."

"These two are my roommates, Will. Meet Mary and Maeve Flaherty, over here from County Clare in Ireland. They work at the Pepperell."

Will stared at the two beautiful young women for a moment, taking note of their braided auburn hair, fair complexions, and gray-green eyes. He was not sure he had ever met such exotic-looking females.

"Pleased to meet you both, ladies," he finally said slowly, as if he had to think about each word before saying it.

Liz noticed that his shyness had returned. He acted much as he had when they met back in the Westbrook boardinghouse.

"Don't be put off by these Catholic belles. They aren't terribly devout in their beliefs."

The three women laughed. Will just blushed and smiled.

53

Arm in arm, Liz and Will returned to strolling around the circular enclosure while the sisters went their own way. At each scene of the Pilgrim's struggle and redemption, the couple stopped and studied as the summer breezes brought life to the painted characters. Liz explained to her willing listener the subtleties of each step in Bunyan's allegory. At the end, when both the Pilgrim Christian and his wife, Christiana, reached the Golden City, Will turned to his lady friend and said, "Miss Liz, thank you so much for explaining all this to me. You have a sensitive eye to the details. I never would have understood ten percent of it except for you teaching me how to look at it."

"Will, I read Bunyan's work this week just so I might make the most of my viewing. The writing is so ancient that it's difficult to understand. Seeing the painted scenes has made it all much clearer. It was good to have a companion like yourself who also appreciates art. My roommates had their fill of it a while ago and would have left me on my own."

"Yes, Miss, I do appreciate the artwork, but only now that you have shown me what it means. Having you to guide me has been wonderful."

As the couple left the barn, Liz spied Mary and Maeve sitting on a wooden bench in the shade of a large elm. They flirted with four young factory boys and ate ice cream from paper bowls. She waved to them, but could not get their attention. She and Will walked over to the group.

"Oo-o-o," said Lizzie, "that ice cream looks yummy."

Maeve, taking the final spoonful from her bowl, stuck out her tongue at Liz with the ice still on it. The four lads laughed loudly. Will stared hard at the girl.

"John and Jake here bought these sweets for us," said Mary.

"So nice of them," returned Liz as these two boys stepped forward and doffed their caps.

"Will has offered us a ride back to the boardinghouse on his uncle's wagon. There just might be room for all of us, if you boys are going that way."

"Wouldn't that make for a grand end to a grand day!" giggled Maeve.

54

Back at work Monday morning, Liz reflected on what an enjoyable outing it had been to Biddeford and how much she had enjoyed Will's company. Nearly three years had passed since she had shared time with a young man. After reading Henry's letter, she had let her fear, like a stone wall, raise itself between herself and every other man of her age. Even though older men like Mr. Webber were kind and helpful, any thought of romance or companionship with a younger man was worrisome.

Moses Webber suddenly appeared at the door. It was unusual for him to show up this early in the morning, even before the other seamstresses were to arrive. His custom was to oversee the arrival of the early shift at the Pepperell before checking on the dress shop's progress with the new fall fashion line. He stood behind her studying the patterns on her drawing table, and she sensed that he was thinking about something before commenting.

She turned to him. He smiled and gently touched her shoulder.

"Liz, your work is remarkable. You have found a way to make those fashion card outfits come to life with a style that is subtly different from the European originals. Our local fabrics are so muted, yet you somehow make them seem much brighter."

"Oh, Mr. Webber, you are so nice to say such things. As I have told you before, a well-made fabric can be used to do many different things. It is my pleasure to use them."

"Lizzie, you have helped to bring greater success to this shop beyond any expectation of myself and the other partners."

He hesitated for a moment, clearing his throat before continuing. "You have also brought a wonderful brightness back to this old man's life."

Setting down her pencil and compass, she stared up at this handsome older man. He wore a gray tweed waistcoat, a striped vest of her design, and a freshly starched white shirt of finest cotton. A wide black silk four-in-hand tie was neatly knotted at his throat.

He went on. "You know that since my wife died six years ago, I have lived alone with the housekeeping help of my cousin. There has been a very dead place in my heart. You, dear Liz, have helped to bring light back into my life once again. I know that I am more than twice your age; but if you have a mind to consider this, I would be pleased to have you as my wife."

A lump formed in Liz's throat. Her heart went a-fluttering. She stood from her work and softly touched his arm.

"Dear Sir, you have already given so much to my life by hiring me to do the work that I love. You have trusted me like a family member, as my own grandfather trusts me. Now you do me a great honor to trust me to share your life. I don't know what to say."

"Lizzie, I know this is a surprise to you. It is such to me, as well. It had been my notion to die a widower. My proposal, nevertheless, is not impulsive; it has grown within my heart and mind for many weeks. Please take the time you need to consider it. If you say yes, you may be assured that you will share fully in my life for the years that remain to me. If you say no, I will regretfully accept that also. It would have no effect on the respect I have for you or our business together."

Liz made an awkward curtsey to him, then took his large hand in hers. He smiled again and walked out the door.

55

Walking home after work, Liz felt better about herself than she had in a very long time, perhaps ever before. Life had given her so many good things in such a short time that it seemed she had found a way at last to a life of happiness and success. Passing several clothing shops on the way, she saw dresses and suits on display that were of her design. A young woman strolled past on the arm of her beau wearing a Webber Co. dress that had been made by her very own hands. Now, within the space of three days, two men had shown her respect of the highest order.

One man had even proposed to her. It seemed her feet hardly touched the ground.

As she entered the door of the boardinghouse, she noticed a letter in her mailbox, grabbed it and noted that it was from Beattie, and because several weeks had passed since the last letter, she added it to a growing list of the good things happening to her. Opening the door to her room, she saw that her roommates had not yet returned from their shifts. She opened the envelope and started to read the letter even before removing her coat and hat. What she read upset her greatly.

Dear Lizzie,

Please forgive me for such a long time between letters. Life here has been very difficult of late. Your grandfather took a very bad fall at the quarry last week. Both his legs are broken, as is his left arm. The rest of his body is severely bruised, especially his back and face. Dr. James—you remember him—has set the splintered bones as best he can and tells me that Hi is lucky to still be alive.

He is now bedridden, as he is likely to be for some time to come. I have been doing the work of us both to keep things going. Hattie and Nathan have come by several times to help me. They are so kind. Neighbors have been in with food for us so that I do not have to cook much. Both boarders have lent a hand with the chores, but there has been little time to sit and write to you.

Hiram himself, God bless him, didn't want me to tell you about the accident, afraid it would upset you. But I had to tell you about the situation. What if he died and I had not let you know what had caused it? You would never forgive me.

I know that you are busy now with your new job, but if you could find the time to return for a short visit, he would be very pleased, I am sure. You have always meant so much to both of us. Perhaps, if you could arrange to get away for the weekend, one of the boarders might be persuaded to meet you at Westbrook station. Bea

Liz fell back on her bed still wearing her coat and boots. She would speak with dear Mr. Webber in the morning about taking leave for this family emergency.

56

As Pay Overseer of the Pepperell, Mr. Webber occupied an office strategically located at the main door where all mill workers would enter and exit the building. There he could hand out pay at the start of each week. He might also be easily able to meet an incompetent worker at the beginning of a shift and dismiss him or her on the spot. Liz knocked softly on the darkly frosted glass door just below his name plate: MR. MOSES W. WEBBER, PARTNER. At first, nobody answered; so she knocked again a bit louder.

"Just a moment there, please. I will be right with you," he said through the door.

Opening the door, he acted quite surprised to see her in his workaday world. Instead of the clothes he had been wearing the previous morning when he had proposed to her, he wore his factory outfit: brown cotton shirt, open at the collar, with sleeves rolled up at the cuff and sleeve garters above each elbow. He wore no jacket, although a gray overcoat hung on a rack behind the door.

"Why, Liz, I hardly expected to see you here at this time of day. And so soon after yesterday's discussion."

She sensed that he was a little bit uncomfortable that she had come; but perhaps that was just because she was uncomfortable about bothering him with her own problems during the workday.

"Have you perhaps reached a decision on my offer? Come in, then. We may talk in private."

Surely, I should not have come here during the shift change, she thought, as he closed the door and led her to a large cushioned bench in front of the dark mahogany desk. He expects my answer now, and I am not ready to decide. He took a seat close beside her.

"Mr. Webber…Moses, I have had so little time to reflect on your proposal. When I arrived home last evening, there was a very distressing letter waiting for me from my grandmother in Westbrook. Grandad has taken a most dreadful fall at work and is now bedridden. My Beattie has asked that I return to see him before, or just in case, he is to die."

Tears flooded her eyes and cut off her words as the possibility of Grandy's death became real to her. Webber took her hand tenderly.

"What can I do to help you through this emergency? Has he a good doctor to care for him?"

"Sir, there is a good doctor there who has already attended to his injuries. I will only need a few days off from work to travel home and return."

"Take what time you need, my dear girl. Can I perhaps provide you with the train fare or a ride to the station in Portland?"

"No, Moses, I have already made those arrangements for tomorrow, hoping you would graciously agree to a short leave. There is enough work for the girls at the shop to keep them very busy until I return. I will send you a letter, once I arrive, to let you know how things are going." She did not want him to worry about falling behind on the new dresses for autumn.

He took her hand once again and led her to the door. She dried her tears with her handkerchief and curtsied to him as before. He assisted her up by the hand, leaned over, and kissed her cheek.

"Be ever careful. Return as soon as you are able—no sooner. Work can wait."

As pleasant as his tone was, she thought she could hear a note of worry about the new line being completed.

57

At the Portland station, Will Cain waited for Lizzie in a brand-new chaise. In the month since their Sunday outing in Biddeford, he had been working six full days a week at James Pride's quarry on Forest Avenue. There was such demand now for cut granite that was being used as curbing and foundations in the rapidly developing East End neighborhood of Portland that Pride and his partners were considering a second shift. Will had been given a new job as foreman of the first shift, but he had gotten the day off because he had volunteered to pick up Lizzie for Beattie.

He looked forward to seeing Lizzie once again. Since he had toured the Pilgrim's Progress panorama in Uncle Luther's barn with her, he had often recalled with great pleasure how she had helped him understand such an ancient allegory. Although this was a sad time for those who still lived at the boardinghouse, that memory brought a smile to his face as he waited.

Liz stepped down onto the platform from the train. She was dressed in an ankle-length blue cotton dress beneath a light-brown tweed coat. A pale yellow bonnet covering her black hair, which was pulled back in a bun, was tied at the throat with a pink bow. He had never seen such a stunning outfit, and his throat tightened as he stared at her.

"Miss Liz! Over here!" he shouted as he jumped down from the chaise. "I volunteered to come for you."

Hesitating for a moment, she seemed unsure who it was who had hailed her. When she recognized him at last in his work clothes and an unshaven face, her expression changed to a smile of relief. She too had looked back on their excursion with happy thoughts. As she approached the carriage, she was thinking about how he had held her arm in his and how respectful he had been toward her, an unusual trait for a young man these days.

"Will Cain, you are a sight for sore eyes. The trip has been so long in such damp weather. The heat of the diesel smoke was horrible. I had no idea how I was going to get out to Pride's Corner."

"I got the day off to fetch you. With all the work now, it is a blessing to have a day off from the heavy machinery, noise, and stone dust everywhere. Since Hiram took his fall..." He stopped himself short, not wanting to ruin their reunion with bad news.

He changed the subject. "Having your company again is today's second blessing."

"So kind of you," she smiled. "So kind to say that. If my visit were not for such a serious purpose, I am sure we might share another stroll. However, since you mentioned Grandy, please tell me what happened to him."

He related how Beattie and the new quarry owners had given Hiram the job of overseeing the storage and packing section of the stone yard in order to keep him out of the more dangerous pits where blasting and excavators had taken the level of operations ten feet below grade. He was directing a crew to load cut stone onto wagons that would transport the heavy loads four miles to Portland. One man stood atop a raised platform running a steam-operated hoist to lift the two- to four-hundred-pound granite pieces onto the wagons. Hiram stood safely off to the side shouting directions when one of the thick canvas slings used to lift the blocks slipped from its hook, flew off, and jammed in one of the hoist gears. The machine made such a loud screaming noise that the two horses pulling the next wagon in line reared up and ran the empty wagon in the old man's direction. In the blink of an eye, the wagon was nearly on top of him. He tried to move aside, but was run over by the front wheels before the teamster was able to bring his horses to a halt.

Liz sat in stony silence next to Will, shocked by the story and unable to speak. She grabbed his arm, put her head against his shoulder, and wept.

"Miss Liz," he said, not knowing how to react to their touching, "perhaps I shouldn't have told you what happened. 'Twould have been best left for you to learn of the accident from your grandma at home. I'm so sorry to have upset you."

She pulled away as if surprised at her closeness to him and dried her eyes with a linen handkerchief. "No, Will. It is good to know the facts from you who were there to witness the accident. Now I am better prepared to face the poor man."

58

She asked Will to let her off at the barn instead of in front of the house. Daylight was quickly fading, and she knew that her grandparents were in the habit of retiring early. She did not want the noise of the horse and chaise stopping by the front door to disturb them if they were asleep already. Entering the door as quietly as possible, she poked her head into the big front parlor, where Beattie sat dozing, reclined in a Morris chair. To the left was a hospital bed on which Grandy lay, his legs inclined slightly in lines of traction. The bed was directly opposite the big fireplace where no fire blazed. A braided rug, the one that had formerly lain across the floor in front of the hearth, was rolled up against the wall, out of the way.

Hiram appeared to be asleep. His head and neck were heavily bandaged, as were both arms. The rest of his body was covered by a white sheet and a blue wool blanket so that his broken legs were not visible except for the white ends of the casts, which stuck out from under the covers. In the stillness, Liz removed her overcoat and bonnet and carefully knelt at his bedside. She bowed her head and prayed for the first time since attending church at Christmas.

Hiram coughed, then woke, surprised to see someone's head beside him. He reached down with his bandaged arm and touched her hair. He was unsure who it was. When he spoke, it was in a very small whisper.

"Who is it that is here? Perhaps you are an angel."

Liz could barely hear the words, so she rose and put her ear close to his face. The smell of medication and rubbing alcohol caused her to back away slightly, allowing him to see her face.

"Oh, Lizzie dear. It is you. I have been waiting for you to return for so long."

"Shhh, Grandy. Beattie is sleeping," she whispered, placing her fingers on his mouth to hush him. His lips were paper dry, and whiskers had grown stubbly around the edges of his bandages. "I have come for a few days to help out. Please don't rouse yourself from sleep; you must need the rest."

Again he whispered, "So hard to sleep. Pain in my legs won't let me get comfortable. Could I have a bit of water?"

She took a full glass from the mantel and held it to his lips as he swallowed. What a sad thing this is, she thought. Here is the strong man who has helped me in so many ways, and now he can't even help himself. Tears started to form in her eyes as she put the glass back, but she was able to hold them for the moment. He smiled up at her and closed his eyes again.

Beattie still slept soundly only six feet away, her breathing deep and regular. Liz walked over to her and straightened the quilt, which was slipping from her lap, so that she would not get a chill. Then the dutiful granddaughter tiptoed from the room, grabbed her bag, and went to her old room just off the kitchen. The light of day would be soon enough to hug and kiss her Grammy. It was then that the tears gushed up from deep within and forced her to lean against the kitchen table lest she fall before reaching the bedroom door.

With the first light of dawn, she was awakened by a knocking at the door. Beattie entered slowly and sat on the edge of the bed. Her face was red with crying and she shook all over as she wrung her hands. Liz had never seen her so distraught.

"He's gone," she said in a trembling voice. "Hi has left us. I just woke and he was cold to my touch." She continued to rub her hands together as if trying to warm them.

Liz said nothing. She threw her arms around her grandmother, moved over to make room for the two of them to lie together on the bed, and covered the old woman with the blanket. Beneath the covers the two cleaved to each other, keening softly with their tears.

59

"How did you know that I was here? Last night when I arrived, you were sound asleep next to his bed," Liz asked as they sat over coffee at the kitchen table.

"You dropped your yellow bonnet on the kitchen floor. Such a fancy bonnet! It had to be yours."

"I must have dropped it when I broke down crying on the way to bed. It was so sad to see him wrapped up in bandages that way. It just didn't seem to be him."

"Yes, Liz, he is better off now. The doctor was so good to him. Stitched and patched him up as best he could, but he was in such pain all the time. I don't think he was able to sleep for more than a few minutes at a time since the accident."

"Will told me how it happened. Why was he still working there? He said he would retire when James Pride bought the quarry."

"He wouldn't give up. Wouldn't stop. We both knew that he had to keep his hand in at work in order to keep this place going. He feared that the new partners would take our house as part of the purchase if we weren't living here. He wanted this place to stay in the family, to be your house, when you came back to live here with us."

Liz stared into her coffee cup for a moment. She did not want to cry again. "He didn't have to die to help me, you know. He should have quit. We could all have dealt with the results. You have all the money I have been sending home since I left two years ago. You could have used that to keep the place running. I am making a good deal of money now working for Webber's. We could have worked things out."

At this, Beattie sighed deeply. "I told him that. You sat with us after Christmas and told us both that same thing. It is just that Hi kept wanting to help you. He wanted you to have that nest egg so you could set up your own business here in Westbrook."

"Grammy," Liz cut her off, "how could he have been so caring about me? Of all the men in my life, he was the only one who ever put me first. My own father never gave a thought to my welfare or to Hattie's. I hated him. Henry Greene stole my heart, gave me hope for the future, only to crush my dreams as if he had never known I existed. Grandy was the best man I ever knew."

She knew she was about to lose control, so she jumped up and ran to her room, slamming the door behind her. Beattie sat in silence. She had not seen her granddaughter this upset since Henry had married that other girl. She said nothing, however, and did not seek to console Liz. The loss of her husband of fifty-five years left such a hole in her heart that she was unable to comfort herself, let alone another.

60

In the fashion of the times, Hiram's funeral was a simple affair. His body was laid in a wooden box placed on a table in the parlor of the house where his sickbed had been located. With the help of Hattie and Nathan, Lizzie draped black crepe paper around the front door and over all of the windows after the curtains were removed. All mirrors in the house were turned to the wall to keep the reflection of light from candles and lamps from brightening the room in which the body lay.

Beattie grieved so deeply that she could not work with the others to prepare for the service. She sat on a stiff wooden chair in the bedroom she had shared with Hiram for so many years. Her life was an empty shell of what it had been with her man. Hattie approached her early on the day of the wake. Both were dressed in black from head to foot. Beattie's head was covered by a veil of black lace, a widow's crown.

"Grammy, please come with me and eat a good breakfast. His friends will be coming soon. It will be a long day. You need to nourish yourself."

"I've no appetite. He has left me. How could he do this? We had agreed to live and die together. He didn't need to be working any longer. Why, Hattie? Why?"

Hattie had no answers, but took her grandmother by the hand to help her stand, then led her down to the kitchen for coffee and toast, which Lizzie had prepared for all of them. As they sat together, Beattie reached out to take the hands of both young women.

"I guess I am carrying on too much. You are still here with

me. I am not alone. Forgive this old lady for being so self-centered, but he was life to me. He made the sun shine."

All three burst into tears.

Nathan entered the room with young Francena, who was dressed in a white dress like an angel. Hattie walked to her, picked her up, and said, "You look so pretty."

Little Franny smiled and said, "Yes, I know. So pretty. So pretty."

Soon they stood on the left side of the open casket, Beattie closest to it. She looked down at the body of her beloved husband for a few seconds, then moved away so that Liz and Hattie could move closer. For the next six hours they greeted a steady line of mourners—friends, neighbors, business associates, and customers of Mr. Hiram Fogg—who came to pay their respects to a man who had made each of their lives a bit better.

At eight in the evening, when the wake was over, Beattie turned to Lizzie.

"Girl, now we know that he was important to more people than us. I never knew he was so loved and respected."

"Gram, he was certainly the most important man in my life. My heart is broken open."

61

Liz stood just inside the door of her bedroom and stared out her window across a wide lawn that separated the boardinghouse from the hubbub of Forest Avenue. There was so much traffic running to Portland and back, it was noisy much of the time—though it was still quieter than Saco. The time had arrived for her to make more decisions about her life, but now it was on her shoulders alone to select a course of action. In the past, she had been fleeing unhappiness in order to improve her life. Now, as she moved closer to the window and sat in a comfortable platform rocker, she realized that she had never before been in a position to decide between two positive options, both of which surely held great promise. In Saco, she had become successful at work, and that made her happy. There were friends whom she loved and who loved her. She even had a marriage proposal to consider. A move back to Westbrook would bring her back to her family and a more rural life, which very much appealed to her. The house would be hers, and there was now a sizable bank account with which she might open her own dress shop.

As she considered the options, she recalled a dream that had come several times recently. In it, she saw herself rise from the very bed she sat next to now, pull a stamped tin trunk from her closet, and empty out all of Marm's belongings stored therein. Then she proceeded to fill the trunk with the remnants of her own life before Henry's letter, mementos that had helped to get her through so many times of tumult.

With the chest sitting at her feet, she first packed her unfinished rosy linen wedding dress, folded neatly and set against the cedar bottom. Then came a quilt handed down from Sewell's grandmother, whom she had met but once, at Marm's funeral. Then she packed away dolls with ragged clothing, some of which she had sewn with her own hands while her mother instructed her. Then followed a number of books, some from childhood with well-worn covers, many others that she had read to the boarders. As the box filled in the dream, Liz felt a weight being taken off her, a burden of remembrance that needed to be thrown aside forever.

She moved faster and faster. There were hundreds of things that needed to be packed in the big chest, and soon it was filled to overflowing. She had to sit on the top and bounce up and down to get the lock closed. Upon waking, her shift was soaked through with perspiration from all the work.

Now, as she sat watching traffic on the road outside, she said to herself, Why have I cherished these remnants of my difficult times? Each time I have looked at that dress, I have bemoaned the loss of love. My dolls have always brought back the grief of Marm's passing. Perhaps it would be better to toss these things in a bonfire.

At that moment she made her decision. She would return to

Saco just long enough to pack her belongings and deliver her answer to Moses Webber. Then she would come back to the family home. She would bring the chest with her and pack all the sad memories in it.

62

Aphia Greene was one of only five people who attended Elizabeth Whitcomb's graveside service in Elm Vale Cemetery where she was interred next to her husband. To the east, the flanks of Bear Mountain were dark evergreen waxed with splashes of autumn color. Its rugged bald face reflected in Bear Pond's still waters. It was a cool, sunny day when the simple casket disappeared into the ground. Reverend Shaw said the final words, assisted by his son, James, who held tightly to him to keep the ancient pastor from falling on the uneven ground. Aphia's brother Ron, now working in a Norway law office, came to represent their parents, who still wanted no part of the daughter who had deserted them. As the burial began, Henry arrived on a horse he had borrowed from a friend in Stoneham, where he had been working in a lumber camp. He had not been "at home" on the farm for nearly six months, and his wife was surprised he had bothered to come. How had he even heard of the woman's passing? she wondered.

"Wife, this leaves you alone on our farm now, doesn't it?" he whispered to her as the pastor prayed over the body. Head bowed, she ignored him. As the rites ended and two diggers began to bury the casket, she started to walk away, hoping that Henry would leave. However, he came up beside her and grabbed her arm.

"Let me take you home, dear," he said loudly, so that the other mourners would hear. "I'm sure there are many chores to be done on the farm, much more than one woman can handle."

Ron, who had been walking toward his sister to express his sympathy, turned away abruptly when he saw Henry latch on to her. He had a lingering affection for her, but disliked her husband so much that he wanted nothing further to do with either of them.

She pulled away from Henry's grip. He laughed and yanked her back to his side. Ron again stepped in her direction, as if to assist her. Henry jumped between them and railed at the young man.

"Leave this woman to me, boy! She is my wife, and I will abide no interference from you or any other of the family. She and I now own that farm outright."

As Ron backed away from confronting Henry, Aphia ran to her brother's side. Both glared at the enraged man before them, unable to gauge whether he might attack. Finally, Aphia stepped forward and placed her hand firmly against Henry's chest.

"Don't you dare to hurt my brother, the only member of my family who cares enough for me to attend Elizabeth's funeral. And don't you dare take your anger out on me, Henry Greene. Do what you want on the farm, but don't count on me to share myself or anything else with you as long as we both shall live."

63

Liz sat on a long cold wooden bench outside the door to Moses Webber's office. The uncomfortable bench had no arms or back. It was a dark day for October with ominous clouds blocking the sun. The shift change at six o'clock approached, and since it was Monday, she knew he would be there to distribute the weekly pay envelopes. She had meant to arrive much earlier in the day, but the journey from Westbrook had been slowed by a series of thunderstorms that made the coach and train travel treacherous. She had hurried from the station direct to the Pepperell even before dropping her duffel at the rooming house.

While she sat waiting, thoughts of what she had to tell Moses ran over and over in her mind. Without a doubt, she would be leaving Saco in a very few days. That decision had been made before leaving Westbrook. Beattie was now relying on her to return and take over management of the boardinghouse—which Liz herself now owned. Transfer of title was already in the works. Yet she did not want to offend the man who had been so good to her, the man to whom she might be wed. Before the events of the past week had caused a drastic change of plans, she had decided to accept the proposal. Now she was not sure what to do. After all, she enjoyed his company, appreciated his respect for her, and looked forward to strengthening their business, as well as personal, relationship as partners. Certainly the prospect of a comfortable life with a man of means and living in his mansion would be a wonderful change…

Moses approached from another office down the hall, and a broad smile came to his face as he realized who it was who sat on the bench.

"Liz, how wonderful it is to see you again. I've sorely missed your radiant smile these last few days."

In his hands were two large gray metal boxes which she assumed held carefully sorted pay envelopes. She opened the door for him, followed behind, and shut the door carefully so that she might speak to him in private. After setting the boxes on a table behind the door, he reached for her hands and swept her into a warm hug. For one so tall and heavy, his caress was very tender.

"I received your wire about your grandfather's death. My condolences to you and your family. Thank you for taking the time to notify me during your time of such grief. There has not been an opportunity to reply, but you might have stayed away from work for a few more days, if you needed to."

"No, Moses, I wanted to return as soon as possible after the funeral. There are, after all, several things we need to speak about."

He looked quizzically at her for a moment and then smiled again.

"Yes, several things, indeed. If it would not be too much of an inconvenience, could I impose upon you to wait here until I have distributed the envelopes? It is just six now. Afterwards we might step out for supper at the hotel and privately discuss our future."

64

Over dinner, she related all that had gone on during her sad visit home. He hardly interrupted except to ask for more details about her family. She kept thinking what a good listener he was and how sincerely concerned he was about her life.

Finally, over coffee, he asked, "Liz dear, have you had a chance to consider my marriage proposal? Unless I am mistaken, this is one of the things we need to discuss—though of course, you have had your mind on other more serious matters."

Taking another sip, Liz sat silently for a moment as she collected her thoughts. "Moses, with my Grandy gone now, you are the dearest man I know." Using the pet name for Hiram brought a catch to her throat. Moses tenderly reached across the table and touched the back of her hand.

She continued, "I would like nothing better than to be your wife. It would be wonderful to live with such a compassionate man as yourself. We already have so much in common, with your business and all. To share a personal life with you would be wonderful."

He held her hand tightly now and stared into her eyes. She knew that he was waiting to hear that she would be his wife, but that he was also aware her answer might be no.

"While my answer to your proposal was to be yes, my experience of the past few days has forced me into making a different decision. Grandma Beattie is sorely in need of assistance at home. I have told you about how helpful they have been to me over the years. I feel that she is my mother. It would be remiss of me to leave her on her own now, even though my desire for a happy married life, like that of my sister, might have to be put off for a while."

As Moses slowly released her hand, she noticed that his eyes were tearing up. He took a white handkerchief from his vest pocket and blew his nose to keep from crying.

"Dear Liz, I feared that your family loss might mean you would be leaving Saco, but now the thought of my own loss has hurt me worse than I expected."

He went on, "I can only hope that we will continue to see each other from time to time. Perhaps you might consider an occasional visit to Mill Town. Or perhaps I might be allowed to visit you in Westbrook once in a while."

She was both surprised and relieved that he had taken her

decision so well. So far, this discussion had gone exactly as she wished. The final part of her plan might well prove to be a stretch of Moses's willingness, but it was worth proposing at this point, while things were going her way.

"Moses, you surprise me. Most men would have reacted in anger at such a denial of their intentions by the woman they love. You are so very sensitive to my need to return to my family."

"Lizzie, if there was only one thing to be learned from my many years of business, it is that in life it is best not to be blinded by personal reactions to the effects brought about by a change in another's circumstances. The death of one so important to you as your grandfather most certainly had to affect our plans."

This time she grabbed his hand tightly. "Moses, you dear man, please accept my gratitude once again. Of course, we can see each other as often as possible, either at your home or in mine. May I also suggest that our visits combine both business and pleasure. When I return to Westbrook, the boardinghouse property will belong to me as Grandy and Grammy wanted. With a sizable nest egg built up at home from the gracious wage I have earned working for you, I plan to convert the first floor into a dress shop similar to yours. If you were to continue to want my original designs for your shop, I could produce those and stay with you here when I deliver them."

Moses looked at her with a thoughtful gaze for the longest moment as he considered her ideas. Then a laugh exploded from him so loudly that others in the restaurant turned to look at them.

"My god, you have a sharp mind for business! Of course, we could try that scheme. You get work. I get exceptional merchandise. We will be able to enjoy each other's company at the same time. How ingenious!"

65

Buoyed by the ease with which Moses had accepted the first part of her plan, Liz returned to her shared room at last to wash away the dust of her journey. She entered the dark room and lit a candle on her bedside table. Neither Mary nor Maeve was in bed. It was likely they had pulled a late shift. A Diamond match and a twist on the wall-mounted gas sconce flooded the room with radiant light.

As she stepped out of her travel outfit and filled a white china basin with wash water from a matching ewer, her gaze wandered about the crowded room. It was larger than her room at the Westbrook house, but with three people sharing it, every available inch was taken up by their belongings, the two beds, and a pair of dressers. There was barely enough space left over for her sewing machine and the tiny secretary's desk and chair she used for fashion sketches. Though she, Mary and Maeve had gotten along very well over their nearly three years together, Liz was ready for a major change in her living situation.

Mary was the first to arrive home, and the two women embraced affectionately, Mary placing a light kiss on her roommate's cheek. Maeve, as was her custom, had likely stayed behind at the mill to chat with one of the young mechanics. While nothing ever seemed to come of her flirtations, she was always willing to giggle, coo, and sometimes offer a kiss. Mary, however, was much different, a cooler person whom Liz often sensed was on edge with men, much as she herself had been until recently. This similarity had drawn the two close together, almost making Liz feel that Mary was like a second sister.

"Lizzie, you're back! So wonderful to see you. I missed you terribly."

As Liz sat on the edge of her bed, she related the events that had happened during her absence in Westbrook. Mary Flaherty was shorter and stouter than Liz, but with her fair complexion and auburn hair, her beauty radiated brightly. Often in the evenings, the three roommates would take turns brushing each other's hair. When Liz took her turn on Mary's curls, she felt very close to her friend.

"Just as I missed you, lovey. Your company would certainly have helped to make my hard time much easier these past few sad days. My Grandy's death is like the end of an age for me. He had always been there for me when things went wrong, and for sister Hattie as well. He rescued both of us from troubled lives following our mother's death."

"Well, girl, you will have to be more there for yourself now, won't ye?" advised Mary. "In Ireland, the funeral of a relative is as much a celebration of a life as it is a sad farewell. Here it is quite different. Your visit sounds very sad indeed. Did you not enjoy the time with your family?"

"Oh, my dear," said Liz, "it was quite sad indeed. Hiram was the head of our family. His loss leaves my Grammy on her own in old age. My sister and her husband are, of course, a great help, but they must travel several hours to get to Westbrook, and they have their own daughter to raise. I was glad to see the family, but it would have been better to share a happier time."

Lizzie's eyes filled with tears again. She took her friend by the shoulders and pulled her closer until they were face to face.

"You know my grief, Mary, and you know my heart. It has been broken before, but this loss will make a stronger woman of me. You will see."

Neither woman was ready for sleep, and when Maeve finally came in, they opened a bottle of port the sisters had stashed away to share at Liz's return. They stayed up late into the night as Liz filled her friends in on all that had happened back in Westbrook. After several tumblers of the wine, she even revealed her new arrangement with Moses.

"Best be careful there," warned Mary.

"Sure you'll be mindin' your manners with an older gent," chimed in Maeve. "He might not have the stamina of a younger man. When Da left us at home, Ma took up with a man nearly twice her age, like your man. Twice she nearly killed him in bed. Be gentle, Lizzie dear!"

Liz held her hand up to Maeve as if to say Stop, you're just being wild again! Then she thought about what the girl was saying. "My god," she said aloud. "What have I gotten myself into? Could something like that really happen?"

Maeve peered quizzically at Liz for a moment, then burst out with, "Heavens, girlie! You're still a virgin, now, aren't ye?"

66

When they finally did go to bed, Liz could hardly sleep as the details of her plans ran through her mind. The lights and night noises out on the streets of Saco, stimuli she had not experienced for the last ten days, also bothered her. Still awake when the others awoke, she jumped from her bed and splashed cold wash water on her face.

"Come on with me to the hotel for breakfast, girls. My treat," she offered.

Off they went arm in arm, almost dancing with each other in the street, while early risers gawked at them as if they were mad. What a mismatched trio they looked. Liz wore a pale blue ankle-length dress of her own design. The sisters had on the white blouses and brown skirts of the factory girl, so that they might be prepared for work later in the day. The hotel waitress didn't know whether to seat them at the counter where factory workers always sat or at the cloth-covered tables in the dining room. Miss Lizzie Millet took charge, and they sat near a big front window where they could watch the busy world go by. Over a sumptuous breakfast of omelets, bacon, freshly squeezed orange juice, and strong coffee, she explained the next part of her plan.

"Grandad has left the big old boardinghouse to me with a stipulation that I must care for Beattie until she passes. Of course, God knows, I would have done that anyway, after what they both did for me. The place is huge. When Hattie and I lived there, we shared a room. Hiram and Beattie had a large apartment, and we had four boarders."

"Will you be taking in boarders now?" asked Maeve. "That will be a lot work for you, then."

"Not at all, Maeve. There is only one man living there now: Will Cain. Oh, you two must remember him. He spent a day with us at the Biddeford exhibit that day."

"Oh, Lizzie, you have had your eyes on that lad for some time!" said Mary.

Liz winked and said, "I am not a two-man woman, dearie. Will has asked to stay on until he finds new accommodations in town. After he leaves, I will be able to turn the street floor into a fancy dress shop with a sewing room in the rear. That has always been my dream. Now Fate has offered me the opportunity. Beattie and I will share the second floor, and my two partners would have the third floor to themselves. It is going to take some hard work to make these changes, but Will has agreed to oversee the renovations to be done by several carpenters he knows."

Mary extended her hand across the table and gave Liz a hearty handshake. "You and your partners will likely be a very busy crew. Touch wood, God will bless your work and you will reach your dream. So few women are able to do something like this. I wish that I might."

"You might, my dear… If you and Maeve will join me as my partners, we will surely be able to succeed. We will all have a much better life for ourselves."

The sisters looked at each other in silence for a moment. Liz said nothing further. Then Maeve let go a cheer that could be heard throughout the dining room and perhaps by those on the street outside the window.

"I'm in!" she shouted. "What say you, Mary?"

"I don't know. It is such a big risk. We aren't even citizens of America. We must talk to the family at home before deciding. They rely so on our regular earnings. Who knows what we will make in this scheme?"

"Don't be a ninny, sister dear! If you had waited for the clan to decide what we wanted to do three years ago, you and I would still be dryin' seaweed and bakin' brown bread in the ashes on the hearth."

Mary peered at her friend, who sat in silence taking another sip of coffee from a fine bone-china cup. In her blue dress, Liz had the look of a very successful businesswoman.

"I want to be like you, Lizzie. You can count us both in on your dream."

67

That night, after the two sisters had gone to bed, Liz sat downstairs in the small parlor. She was so excited about the ease with which her plans for the future were unfolding that she was unable to sleep, preferring to sit up and make notes in her daybook about next steps. Occasionally, a fellow resident returned from a late shift and gestured good night to her, but she was so wrapped up in planning that she didn't notice them.

While things are going my way, she thought, I want to act quickly so I don't lose my momentum. Mary and Maeve must give acceptable notice at the Pepperell so as not to upset Moses and his other partners. I am free to head home as soon as arrangements can be made. I have very little to pack up. Most of my belongings can be securely left in the big Webber house. My sewing machine, some clothes, and a few other essentials may be carried in Marm's and my big trunk.

A list of things to do was made for the Irish sisters. A long list of jobs to be discussed with Will and his carpenters covered two pages. There would likely be permits and paperwork to be processed through the Westbrook Town Office, but she, as the owner, would have to handle those details. There was also a list for Moses; it was the most difficult to compile. She had never lived with a man other than her Grandy, so she was unsure that she would be able to ask her new partner to make a place for her that would be to her liking. Would he think her too pushy if asked him to give her a room of her own? With both business and personal items to be balanced on this list, it was not surprising that it took until the rosy dawn of a new day to complete it.

Quickly climbing the stairs and quietly opening her door, she saw that both sisters still slept soundly in their bed. While washing her face and combing back her curls, she wondered if they would continue to sleep together even after her own bed went empty. That thought brought a big smile to her face, and she nearly burst out laughing.

She tiptoed out of the room, exited the boardinghouse, and rushed along the newly paved street to the hotel, where a cup of black coffee and a piece of buttered toast with local blueberry jam provided a quick boost of energy to start the day. There was so much to be done.

At the dress shop, which had not yet opened, a few design tools—rulers, compass, pattern paper, and drawing pencils—were packed in a large portfolio along with sketches of current projects. Laid on top of these was her shop uniform, an ankle-length cotton duck work jacket stained with ink and stuck with dozens of common pins.

She hurried next to the Pepperell, where it was her hope to greet Moses as he arrived to oversee the morning shift change. Instead, one of his assistants stood at the front door. Moses, it turned out, had taken the day off in order to "prepare for a guest," as the young assistant put it.

Liz had only been to the Webber house twice before—once to retrieve some fabric and most recently for a Sunday lunch. It was not the grandest house in Saco, but its location on Pool Street at the corner of Elm was just elevated enough to allow for a view over the river beyond Mill Island and up to the wider Saco Falls. The pathway up to the front of this center-entrance raised cape was lined with a lovely garden designed by the late Mrs. Webber and still maintained in the original style by several Italian gardeners.

At her first knock, the door swung wide open. Moses stood there dressed in his regular work clothes, a large broom in his big hands.

"My dear, I saw you coming up the path. So delightful to see you at the break of day."

"Yes, yes, I thought to catch you at the mill. There are a hundred things to discuss with you. Our plans are so exciting! I want to have them all happen so quickly!"

"Liz, you surely are full of the energy that comes with youth. Come lend a hand in cleaning a quiet room just for yourself. I asked my cousin to prepare it, but she refused, saying that if I was going to keep a new woman in the house, I could just take care of it myself."

Lizzie stopped short on the top step. "No, I don't want to be the cause of driving her away."

"Don't fret. She is family, after all, and has worked here since my wife died. She is only off to her own home to spend the day with her family in Biddeford. She will return in due time. We must realize there will be some adjustments to be made to our new arrangement, both by others and ourselves. Rest assured she will be back soon enough."

He reached out for her hand and drew her into the foyer, where they embraced. Liz loved the way he wrapped his strong arms around her. It made her feel so safe and loved. When he began to stroke her hair and planted a kiss on her forehead, she reached her arm around the back of his neck and returned a passionate kiss on his lips. They held each other tight for a moment until Moses broke the spell.

"We'd best get on with preparing that bedroom for you."

68

In the days that followed, Liz busied herself with all that had to be done before leaving for home. Clothes, bedding, and three boxes of her things were moved to what would soon be her new Saco residence. Another month's rent was paid to her landlady so that Mary and Maeve would have the room to themselves as they made their own moving arrangements. The chest was packed and transported to the train station.

As she boarded the B & M liner for the short trip to Portland, her mind was so set on reaching Westbrook that she failed to notice Will Cain sitting several rows behind her. As the train squealed and puffed away from the platform, he stepped up next to her.

"Miss Lizzie," he greeted her, "I am surprised to run into you here."

"Will…oh my God, Will Cain. What a pleasant surprise. I was just thinking of you. How wonderful!"

She moved over and made room for him to sit next to her on the bench. He was so very handsome, dressed as he was in a light wool travel suit. Though not wearing a tie, his waistcoat was buttoned to the top just as his white shirt was buttoned to the throat. As he sat, she gave his hand an affectionate squeeze.

"I've been visiting my uncle again in Biddeford. He has been quite ill with influenza. On my way back to the station, I stopped by your dress shop, but an older gent there told me you had left to return home."

"Imagine—we are on the same train," she said. "I was wondering what I might do on the journey. Now I know. There are some things we might want to discuss."

69

At Beech Hill Farm, Aphia constantly lived on edge. Henry had decided to move back home now that both of her grandparents could no longer keep an eye on him. When he took possession of the second-floor bedroom, she moved into the former old folks' room just off the winter kitchen, behind the hearth and beehive oven. She put a bolt on the door and kept it locked every night, afraid even to leave the room to use the outhouse. During the day, when she cared for the horses and did her other chores, she was keenly aware of him watching her every move.

One day, when she was on her knees pulling weeds from the herb garden, he came silently up behind her. He grabbed her rear end and pushed her body onto the ground. He threw himself on top of her, took hold of her shoulders and turned her over on her back. With all her strength, she seized his head and pushed his face into some purple flowers. With the three-toothed cultivator in her gloved hand, she raked his chest, ripping his shirt and opening a large gash in his left side. Henry bellowed, rolled over, and removed the tool that was stuck in his flesh. Blood ran from the wound, which was smeared with flowers and bits of green leaves from the monkshood.

"Damn you, woman!" he cursed. "How dare you! You've

nearly killed me!" he screamed as he thrashed around amongst the flowers.

In response, she growled, "You touch me again and I will slice more than your chest, you bastard. Keep your hands off me. We may be married by law, but the last thing I want is to spend the rest of my life with you. It was good when you were away. Why don't you leave again?" She shook with anger that he would have tried to rape her.

"You'd like that, wouldn't you? Well, it ain't gonna happen!" he shouted as he jumped up and headed to the pump where he could wash the wound. "I am here permanently. You best get used to that. This place is mine, and I will be staying for the rest of my days."

He stopped for a moment and gave a dark and sinister laugh. His face had flushed a bright red. "Hey, girlie, why don't you go back to your family in Norway, if they will let you. Or is that bridge already burned?" Again he chuckled.

Aphia came to her feet, but was in such shock that she lost her balance and toppled again onto the herb plants she had been weeding. Looking down, she saw that her gloved hand was solidly planted atop the beautiful purple flowers of the monkshood. Elizabeth had warned her about the poisonous properties of the plant, especially its root. Small amounts of the leaf had helped her cure a minor cough and relieve her monthly cramps. Perhaps a larger amount might help solve another of her problems…

70

Upon arrival in Portland, Will shouted out to a friend who awaited with a borrowed quarry wagon. The men transferred Liz's big trunk from the platform onto the wagon bed. She took a seat next to the stranger on the front bench while Will sat behind on the trunk. The man looked familiar to Liz, but a full beard hid his features.

Will introduced them to each other. "Liz Millet, this is Bert Learned. He is a man from Waterford who has just started working with me. Bert, meet Miss Lizzie Millet."

Liz and Bert looked at each other for a moment in silence until she smiled and reached out a hand to shake his. "Bert, it has been so long. How have you been?" she began. "How is that farm of yours in East Waterford?"

Will was shocked. "You two know each other?"

Bert spoke in a quiet, shy manner. "Miss Lizzie, you have grown to become a very beautiful woman."

71

On the way to Westbrook on Forest Avenue, Bert relaxed as he and Liz entertained Will with stories of the early days in Hiram and Beattie's boardinghouse. Bert reflected on how enjoyable those times had been when Liz would read stories to the boarders after dinner each night. No mention was made of Henry Greene, however, until they approached Pride's Corner.

"Bert, whatever happened to your good friend Henry? I know he bought a farm in West Waterford, but I never heard how he made out there," Liz said.

"Well, he did get a nicer place than he expected up on the south flank of Beech Hill. Two hundred acres, I recall. The old Whitcomb place it was. He married a young Norway girl. He and I have really lost track of each other. My farm is in the east part of town on the north falls of Long Pond, the south end of which you know. Kind of far from Beech Hill."

She did not press for any more details, fearing that Bert might know more about this matter, including her own sorry part in it, which she wouldn't want Will to know.

"Miss," said Bert, "there was a story about that you were going to move to Waterford. I doubted that one from the start."

Will sat in silence as they conversed, contemplating how much common history his friends might share, but not wanting to pry. Then he reached out and placed his hand on her shoulder. "Miss Liz, you have been away in Mill Town for so long. I remember when I took you to the station that first time. It is good to have you home where you belong, where you have always wanted to be."

72

Rising from her interrupted weeding, Aphia removed her gloves and brushed the dirt and leaves from her clothes. Anger at what Henry had done brought her to consider how to get rid of him. She was thinking of ways to poison him as she walked toward the pump to clean her hands. He was still at the well where he had gone to clean up, but he was leaning against the pump as if having a problem standing.

As she approached, he turned toward her. His eyes were puffy and bloodshot. On the left side of his face, a dark red rash had quickly risen. She saw that he hadn't even had the strength to raise the pump handle and get water to wash his wounds, which continued to bleed all over his shirt, pants, and boots. No words came from his lips as they moved until, with the greatest of effort, he forced out in a whisper: "You witch. You have done this to me. You have rubbed some poison into the cut."

He fell face first to the muddy ground around the wellhead, rolled onto his side, and lay there with eyes bulging wide open. His last words were "Damn you."

She didn't know what to do. Thoughts of killing the man with poison had been in her mind, but murder was a sin—not something she would actually do. However, it seemed that her wishes had been granted: he was now out of her life. First, thoughts of relief came to her, then fears of having done a godawful thing. What would happen now? Would she be arrested? Maybe the body should be buried so that no one but herself would ever know what happened. Yes, yes, he was always away. Never home. He just left and never come back. Yes, that was what she would do.

Although his body was heavy, she was strong enough to drag it along the ground. It took a while, but within an hour, she had managed to move it along the cart path that led to the closest pasture, to the spot where her first horses had been struck and killed by lightning. First she pulled on his hands, but since he was face down, his boots caught on rocks and roots in the path. Finally she was able to roll the body over onto its back and tie a rope around its legs. Still the going was slow. Sight of the rash-red head bouncing up and down on the rocky ground nearly made her throw up. She finally went to the barn and got one of the horses from its stall, saddled it, and rode it to the well. She tied the rope to the saddle horn, mounted, and guided her steed toward the mass grave her grandfather had dug years before.

With a sharp spade, a large shallow hole was dug to the depth where she reached well rotted horseflesh. The stench of the long-buried animals made her sick in the stomach. She puked into the new grave. Then she rolled Henry's body into the hole, doused it with lime, and covered it with dirt. Sweat saturated her clothes as she returned the horse to its stall with the others. Then her strength failed her at last and she fell onto the ground and cried until she had no more tears in her.

73

Liz, Will, Bert, and Beattie sat around the kitchen trestle table. These four remaining boardinghouse residents now ate their meals in that smaller setting instead of at the big dining room table that could seat twelve. Beattie, although in her eighty-first year, still cooked the evening meals, usually a simple stew, chowder, or other one-pot dish. This night's dinner, with her granddaughter's assistance, was like those of days gone by: a roast chicken, biscuits, boiled turnip, and baked potatoes.

"Mrs. Fogg, you've outdone yourself tonight," said Bert as he buttered his vegetables. "Maybe we could get Lizzie to stay around. Then we might eat like kings every night. Maybe we could get Hattie back here, too. They could read to us again."

"Not much chance of that happening, Bert. She is over in Bridgton now with a family of her own to entertain," said Liz.

Beattie hardly touched her food. She sat lost in thought as

the others ate. After dinner, as she and Liz washed the dishes, she began to sigh loudly.

"Lizzie, I'm concerned about your sister. You know, of course, that she is carrying her second child. She's been pregnant for nearly four months. The last delivery was so difficult that her doctor has her staying in bed or lying on the sofa much of the day. They do not want her taking any risk of losing the baby or doing more damage to herself."

"Have you seen her lately, Grammy?"

"No; the trip is too long for me now, and she's been wanting to stay home."

"I'll go see her as soon as we get work started for the shop. She has always been there for me in my hard times."

74

Next morning, she and Will met in the parlor to discuss the remodeling project. They worked very well together, and within an hour, the scope of the work had been roughly laid out. The parlor and dining room at the front of the first floor would become the sales and display area. The summer and winter kitchens would be combined into a weathertight year-round work space where a design cubicle could be set up for her, as well as two work areas for seamstresses. The central stairway would lead up to a second-floor apartment where she and Beattie would reside. It would include a small eat-in kitchen, a modern bathroom, and two generous bedrooms. The third floor would have two small bedrooms and a bathroom for the Flaherty sisters. Bert entered the room at one point, saying that he might be helpful in working up a budget for time and materials because he had done so several times at his farm in Waterford.

Liz lay on the worn velvet sofa, removed her shoes, and stretched her long legs out across the cushions. She noticed how both men glanced at her stockinged feet, their discussion interrupted.

"Haven't you boys seen a girl's ankles before? Perhaps I might go put on a pair of galoshes to make you more comfortable."

Bert was the first to respond. "You have something about your look and ways that reminds me of my Winifred. She was such a lovely soul."

Will turned to him. "You've not told me before about your wife."

"It's not the kind of thing that comes up in conversation very often for me. Both she and my boy perished when our house burned down six winters ago. I was off in Stow working at a logging camp. When I returned to find the place a ruin and the two bodies stored in a mausoleum for spring burial, I turned to drink and lost the farm."

Liz sat bolt upright, jumped from her seat, and hugged Bert with such force that they both nearly toppled over. Will, not knowing how to act at such news, simply patted his friend on the back.

75

Relieved that the work was in such good hands, Liz came to Beattie's room the next morning and said, "Grammy, come with me to Bridgton. You'll be in the way here. Come, let's go visit Hattie. I've arranged for a chaise with a full roof to shade you. We'll be there in three or four hours' time. Won't you be a blessing for my sister and her girl!"

"No, no; it is far too long a trip for the likes of this old lady. Besides, there's work to do cleaning and moving furniture."

"You think an old woman will be a help in doing the heavy work? It's not for the likes of us two ladies. Let the lads do it all. We can go off for an adventure."

Beattie could resist no longer, so the next morning, just after dawn, the two set off on Bridgton Road. A bit of fog still lay across Highland Lake in Westbrook. Pride's Quarry, too, looked much like a bowl full of cotton candy. As the morning sun burned away low clouds, Liz drove the horse faster westward through Windham and then Casco, along the east shore of Sebago Lake. At the Naples causeway, they stopped to rest, peering northward toward Bridgton and the Oxford Hills. The naked peaks of Mt. Washington and the other White Mountains radiated in the sun over the far end of Long Lake. As they continued on to the west, Pleasant Mountain's triple humpbacked ridge soon appeared clearly across meadows and pastures. By the time they crossed a bridge over Stevens Brook and came to Main Street in Bridgton, Beattie had been asleep for over an hour, wrapped in a heavy wool blanket.

Little Francena played in the yard of Hattie's house on South High Street. She ran around the lawn pulling a red wagon in which several dolls rode. The girl did not notice the horse-drawn wagon approaching until Auntie Liz cried out, "Hello, sweetie!" At that, Franny ran to the gate in the picket fence. She opened the gate, then pulled the wagon out to the street.

Beattie, now wide awake, brightened up with a glowing smile. "It's your Grammy, come to visit, Franny."

Liz jumped down from the chaise and secured the horse's bridle to a granite hitching post. As she helped Beattie down, Franny began to scream with delight. She had not seen much of Aunt Liz for some time and did not recognize her right away, but Grammy, who had been a regular visitor until recently, had always delighted her by bringing picture books and candy. The commotion brought Hattie to the porch. She was pale and wrapped in a heavy shawl, but the sight of her two favorite people in the world brought tears to her eyes and a huge smile to her face. The scene of an old lady wrapped head to foot in a blanket, a tall attractive woman wearing a lovely riding outfit, and an obviously ill woman in nightgown and slippers, all hugging and kissing while a little girl pulled a red wagon in circles around them, must have been a joyous sight to passersby.

When the excitement had finally calmed, Beattie and Francena went indoors to nap. The sisters sat together in the parlor with logs aflame on the hearth. Hattie lay on the sofa with her head propped up on pillows. She said very little, but listened intently to all of Liz's stories and plans.

After a while, the younger sister commented, "Lizzie, my

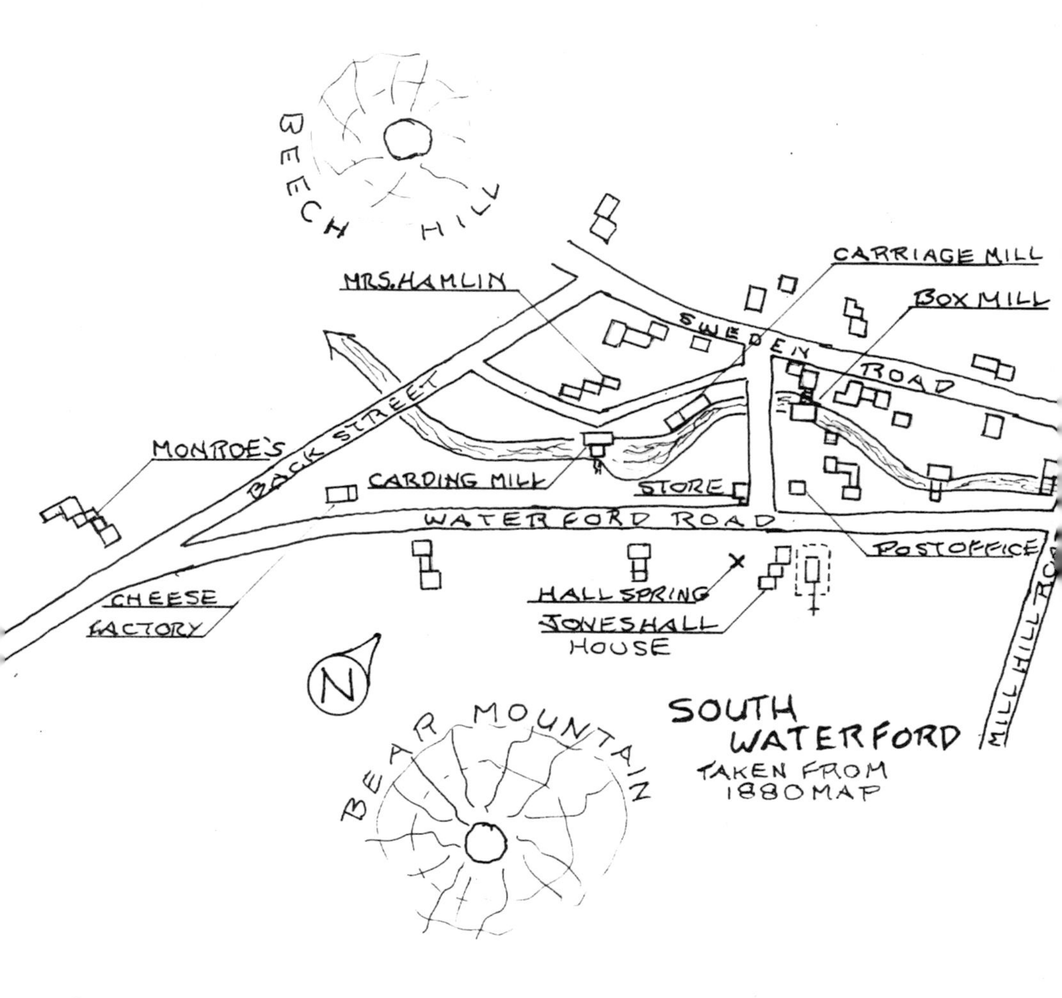
BEECH HILL
CARRIAGE MILL
BOX MILL
MRS. HAMLIN
SWEDEN ROAD
BACK STREET
MONROE'S
CARDING MILL
STORE
WATERFORD ROAD
POSTOFFICE
CHEESE FACTORY
HALL SPRING
JONESHALL HOUSE
N
BEAR MOUNTAIN
SOUTH WATERFORD
TAKEN FROM 1880 MAP
MILL HILL ROAD

dear, your life is so full, so exciting. Each day must be like a new adventure to you. The decision to leave Westbrook and to seek your fortune in Saco must be the best decision either of us has ever made."

"Wait, Hattie, love. You have such a full life of your own. I have often prayed that God would send me such a wonderful man as a husband and partner. Look at your beautiful girl. She must delight you."

"Yes, I know I am blessed; but somehow it seems that the best years of my life are behind me. Nathan is a good husband, yes, but in order to support us, he is away so much of the time. And yes, Francena is my darling. Yet even now, as I wait for another darling to arrive, my body hurts from the work of bearing children."

Liz moved from her chair to sit on the floor beside her sister. Hattie began to smooth Lizzie's hair as she had done in childhood.

"Do you remember that afternoon after Marm's funeral, when we sat on the front porch looking across the fields down to Long Pond behind our schoolhouse?" Liz asked in a quiet voice.

"Oh, yes. We were waiting for Beattie and the others to decide our fates. We spoke of running away together. I remember it as if it was only yesterday.

Liz grabbed Hattie's hand, placed a tender kiss on its palm, and pressed her head against her sister's arm, grabbing it so tightly that Hattie drew back in surprise.

"Hattie, my love, we have done so much better than we might have if we had run away that day in Waterford. There may be problems still, but we have shaken off so many of our demons."

Neither woman wanted to let go. They sat in silence until the coals in the fire failed to give them any warmth. As they went off to bed, Liz decided that a short journey back to Waterford might be just the thing for tomorrow. Hattie was reluctant to join in because of her doctor's advice. However, as they kissed good night, she said that she would make up her mind in the morning.

76

Hattie's decision to accompany her sister on a trip to Waterford set off a family row. Beattie was dead set against the idea. Not only was such a journey against doctor's orders, it would also leave her alone in charge of the little girl for as long as her mother was gone.

"No, you can't do this," the old lady said firmly. "If Nathan were here, he would forbid you to go. Heaven help us if anything happens out there in the wilderness and you need medical care. There isn't a good doctor to be found anywhere near that place."

"Grammy, please listen to me," said Hattie. "The town is only a short distance from here. We will only go if the weather is mild. The trip will only take a morning at the most."

"I don't care. It is a foolish undertaking. Hiram is probably turning in his grave right now with worry."

Lizzie finally stepped forward and put an arm around the old lady's shoulders. "Gram, we are going back to where we started, whether you approve or not. I will keep a careful eye on Hattie and turn back directly if there seems to be a problem, no matter how small. We will be away only one night and will return on the second day early for supper. Fear not. Waterford is not a wasteland, a Lebanon on the other side of the world."

Her younger sister added, "And I will leave food for you and Franny. There'll be no need of you doing any extra cooking. Please calm yourself. There is, after all, no stopping us."

Beattie was resigned to their insistence. "Just remember, your grandfather is no longer around to rescue you girls again."

77

It was a cool morning for the middle of May when the sisters set out. Liz hitched the Morgan to her borrowed wagon and raised the canopy fully open to protect them from sun, wind, and dust. Hattie, overdressed in a heavy sweater and overcoat at Beattie's insistence, climbed up beside her on the leather seat. A basket with extra clothing, lunch, and water sat between them. A bright sun rose and the weather turned quite warm as they drove up High Street toward Bridgton center. Maples and dogwoods were just beginning to bud out.

At the Civil War monument, they turned to the right, downhill toward the town center. Farmer Hastings, from whom Liz had borrowed the horse, had given her a hand-drawn map of the eight-mile route. There were several other ways to get to Waterford, but he had suggested that the route on Harrison Road would offer the easiest grades. As they left town, heading to the north, the sun dimmed as it rose through a thick fog bank at the foot of Pleasant Mountain to the west.

"What beautiful farmland," Hattie remarked. "I have forgotten how pastoral the area is. I can't remember going to Bridgton much as a child. We were in Harrison once in a while, but not way out this way."

"Hattie dear, back in the war times, people never traveled very far from home. I can barely remember going to Waterford Flat, and it is only a mile or so from our old house. How things have changed. Two women would never have ventured out on their own."

On they rode up a long incline where the waters of Long Lake began to appear through trees just beginning to show signs of green. As they topped the rise and began to descend, roofs of buildings in Harrison appeared across open plowed fields and pastures of grazing milk cows. When the lake came up close to them at Kimball's Landing, they turned to the left onto North Bridgton Road and through the lovely campus of Bridgton Academy.

"Sister, do you remember the book of Emerson's poetry which you gave to me when I left for Saco? Ralph Waldo Emerson went to school right here many years before we were born. I still have that volume. You wrote inside, 'An old book with new ideas.' I could never part with that. It is so dear to me."

On the road beyond North Bridgton village, the land quickly became even more rural. Pastures and cultivated fields lined both sides of the road, but on the left, these were backed by tall pine groves and a rugged hillside. To the right, green pasture ran unbroken down to Bear River. Except for rough stone walls and occasional rail fences, there was no sign of human habitation until they spotted a small farmhouse in the distance across the river, next to the marsh at the foot of Hawk Mountain's naked granite face.

"We're almost at Bear Pond and the foot of Bear Mountain," said an excited Hattie.

When they came to the end of North Bridgton Road, where it joins with Waterford Road, Liz pulled the carriage off onto the verge. The bare crag of Bear Mountain rose majestically to the right out of a stand of tall pines and a field of large boulders. Tranquil waters of the pond spread like a dark mirror off to the left, reaching pine-blanketed hills atop which lay open pastures and white farmhouses. It was the very spot they had come so many times as children to swim. And often they had sat high up on the rocky cliff edge that bordered the Hamlin family's farm and stared out across the dark blue waters.

"Hattie, let's stop here to rest and eat lunch. I am tired from the drive. The peace of this spot will bring me rest. Before we reach the village, we would do well to pause and collect ourselves."

They climbed down from the bench, took off their boots, and waded in the cool water just as they had done as children. Hattie turned to Liz and said, "You, especially, will need your strength to revisit a place with such difficult memories—much more difficult than mine, I'm sure. I had already left before Grandy had to rescue you from Father and Rose. Then there was Henry Greene…"

78

In silence, they sat and ate lunch on a little sandy beach where the pond flowed south to enter the river. Then they climbed back on the wagon and drove on toward South Waterford village. Just past the pond's north shore, several wagons and horses were tied up at a big white house and barn that might have been a hotel or inn. Next along the way was a long two-story barn or industrial building on which hung a sign saying WATERFORD CHEESE.

Liz was sure they had entered the village center because she recalled the cluster of white buildings as they rode in. The Universalist Church sat above the road, resting at the base of Mill Hill. Next to it was the small cape where Mr. Hall, a good friend of the Foggs, lived, and the nearby spring where Grandy had watered his horse that day when he had rescued her from Rose.

A small store now sat across Waterford Road from Hall Spring with a tiny hand-lettered sign on its pine board door: GRANGE STORE. Leaving Hattie on the wagon bench, Liz jumped off and made her way toward the store. She leaned against the door to open it and entered what looked and smelled like a cattle stall. Cloth bags were stacked along the rear wall nearly floor to ceiling. Kernels of corn mixed with brown grains and seeds littered the floor around these sacks. At her left, a man sat at a low workbench making shoes.

"Good day, miss," he said. "Such a nice spring day to be out and about, I'd say."

"And you would be right to say that," she joked.

"What can I do for you this fine day? I don't believe for a moment that a fine lady such as yourself would be looking to buy any seed."

"No. My sister, who is out on the wagon, and I have returned to South Waterford for a visit and are hoping to find a room for the night."

"Returned, you say. Returned from where? You've been here before?"

"My name is Lizzie Millet. My sister Hattie and I grew up on the Millett farm up on the top of Mill Hill Road at Skunk Alley, near to the Hamlin place."

"Hello! Hello!" said the gent as he rose from his bench and dusted off his apron. "Are you the granddaughter of Hiram Fogg? I thought I recognized your features. I am Jones Hall, not that you would remember me. How is old Hiram?"

She informed Hall that his good friend had recently passed

on and that Beattie, whom the man had met many times, was still living in the big Westbrook boardinghouse. Then she walked back to the open door and shouted to Hattie, "Come in and meet Mr. Jones Hall, the cobbler who made your boots for Bethel."

79

Hall entertained them for an hour or so with stories of many things that had happened in South Waterford in the years since Liz had been rescued. He told about the way in which William Watson, the box mill owner and town selectman, had sent Rose Millet home that fateful morning to take care of her abandoned babies. And how the selectmen eventually took the children away from their parents and found a safer home for them with another family in town—Reverend Shaw and his wife. When Liz asked him about Henry Greene, he spoke of the first few weeks after Greene had arrived in West Waterford—how he wed a young girl and treated her unkindly even while her grandparents were still alive and living with the couple on the family farm.

"Is he still living in town?" asked Liz.

"I'm not quite sure. He's around the village once in a while. I see him over at the post office occasionally, but I hear he was working for a while over in Vermont on a dairy farm owned by his uncle. I know the girl still has the farm. Has some horses she's raising. She's sort of gone crazy up there, on her own most of the time."

"Did she have any children with him?" asked Hattie.

"Not that I know of. Some say that she was pregnant early on. I'm not sure of that myself. They never got along too well, especially after both Abe and Elizabeth Whitcomb died. The grandmother has only been gone for a few months now. But I think the girl is alone, at least most of the time, up on Beech Hill with her horses."

Realizing that the light was fading and that they needed a room, Hattie said, "Mr. Hall, I thank you very much for being so welcoming to strangers from away. If it suits you, might we be able to come back tomorrow and chat a bit more before we leave? Right now we need to find a place to stay."

"Well, there's always Mrs. Monroe's place. You passed it at the head of Bear Pond. Or the Houghton House Hotel up on Sweden Road. The W. K. Hamlins also have a nice little room to let just beyond the Crossways Bridge, across from their carding mill. You may know W. K. He grew up on Skunk Alley right next to your old place. I know that Mrs. Hamlin is home. She was just here with me this morning. If you check in at the mill, Mr. Hamlin will help you out."

Walking down the dirt road next to Hall's store, Liz led the horse with Hattie walking behind. As they crossed the old split granite bridge over City Brook, loud machine noises emanated from Watson's box factory. They could barely hear themselves talk above the din. At the left hand turning onto a very muddy road, another mill building, set back against the stream, accosted them again with loud noises. Screams emanating from some sort of grinder spooked the horse. Under a wheelless wagon up on wooden blocks, two men lay on the ground with a device that shot showers of sparks into the air above their work area.

The roadway was lined with stacked logs, empty barrels made of both wood and rusting metal, lying on their sides, rusty gear wheels, and piles of debris. Chickens ran and pecked along the road verges. A lopsided shed leaned precariously against a small barn where goats licked at what grass remained. A hundred feet ahead, they saw a single-story cape-style building, shingled on its gable but clapboarded on the front. This third rustic manufactory contributed its own sounds to the rumbling and whirring of the neighborhood.

"My God, Lizzie, what an awful racket" shouted Hattie. "How can folks who live in that cute white house across the road put up with such noises? I would be driven mad!"

"People grow used to the din," Liz answered. "In Saco, I sometimes didn't even notice all the factory sounds. I'll bet it is quiet here at night when the work stops. Down in Milltown, work went on night and day. Seldom did it stop."

At the carding mill, a gentleman dressed in a neat suit of homespun wool stepped out to stand at the top of a set of split granite steps. This had to be Mr. W. K. Hamlin. In his dress and manner, he reminded Liz of Moses Webber, although he was much smaller. He stood quite erect as he waved to them. She could tell that he was in charge of the operation.

Mr. Hamlin directed the sisters to his wife, who sat on the long porch of the family residence just across the way. She led them to a side entrance and up a set of stairs to a comfortable bedroom above a garage. There was only one big double bed, but the two decided that, even though they had not slept together for twenty years or more, such a clean and bright room would do very nicely.

"My two partners, Mary and Maeve, have been sleeping together their whole lives," said Liz. "It seems to keep them close." They both laughed.

Hattie giggled. "I'm sure it does."

"No. No—you know what I mean. It makes them feel so close to each other."

80

Liz and Hattie woke early for the trip home. In truth, neither of them slept very well, being so excited about their adventure. The sun had barely broken over the tops of the tall pines to the east on the slopes of Bear Mountain. As they dressed, a quiet knock came to the door.

"We are up and dressed," said Hattie as she turned the knob.

It was Mrs. Hamlin. "Didn't want to disturb you, but I thought I heard footsteps up here. There's someone here who wishes to speak with Miss Lizzie. She says that you do not know her, but that she has heard much about you."

Peering out the window, Liz spied a beautiful young woman feeding grass to a handsome Morgan. The woman's short, roughly cropped hair reached barely to her ears so that her stunning facial features were clearly visible. A riding outfit of denim pants and a smart plaid jacket showed off her figure. In an instant, Liz guessed it to be Aphia, the girl for whom Henry had thrown her aside. A catch came to Liz's breathing as she saw how much more beautiful the younger woman was than she herself. Then she remembered from what Mr. Hall had told them that beauty alone had perhaps not brought happiness with it.

"Mrs. Hamlin, please tell our visitor that we will be down shortly for breakfast. Perhaps with your kind permission she might be able to join us at table."

When they reached the dining room, they found a hearty breakfast of eggs, toast, and coffee set for them. There was a third place set at the table, but the chair remained empty. Mrs. Hamlin approached as they ate. She spoke in a tense whisper directed at Liz, as if she did not want Hattie to hear the message.

"Miss Liz, the girl's name is Aphia Greene. She says that she does not wish to share breakfast with you, but would appreciate it if you might speak alone with her for a moment outside."

Sensing her host's discomfort, Liz left her sister to breakfast, put on her warm cardigan, and stepped outside to meet the stranger. She strode boldly up to Aphia and put out her hand. The younger woman, surprised that another woman might seek to greet her in such a masculine manner, hesitated for a moment before extending her own hand and shaking Liz's weakly.

Liz began, "Aphia Greene, I am Liz Millett."

"I know very well who you are, miss. Mr. Hall told me that you were here in the village. Come to check up on your Henry, I presume," she said in a confrontational tone of voice.

"No, dear. My sister and I have come to visit our own childhood neighborhood. Henry has nothing to do with my life anymore."

Aphia pulled roughly on her horse's reins. It snorted loudly and moist snot from its nostrils sprayed her face. In an attempt to compose herself, the young woman stepped back and straightened her jacket.

"Miss, I have known for some time that you and my Henry were to be wed. He told me that he had promised to bring you to my granddad's farm, where the two of you might raise a family. It has always bothered him something horrible that he abandoned you. In a way, it has ruined his life and my life, also."

Speechless for a time, Lizzie studied the beautiful young

lady before her. Although Aphia was the woman who had taken Henry and dreams of happiness away, she could not blame her. It was Henry who was at fault. The girl was only an element of his cruelty. The anguish and long-term melancholy that had overwhelmed her during the abandonment flashed through her mind and sent a chill down her body.

"Why do you not speak, miss?" Aphia yelled. "You are lucky to have been thrown aside! I took your place and have suffered for it each day since then. My family abandoned me when I ran away with him. Father cursed me and said I was dead to him. Now I am left alone with no one to help me get along on that farm."

Pacing back and forth in a rage beside the horse, its reins still held in her hand, she began to throw her free hand wildly in the air. The nervous animal reared up, pulling itself free, and set off at a gallop toward the carding mill.

Liz took hold of the girl's arm, thinking it might calm her down. Instead, Aphia pulled away and swung her fist at Liz's head. A sharp blow knocked Liz to the ground, where she lay in shock for a moment. Mrs. Hamlin, hearing the shouting, rushed from the house.

Missus Greene! Miss, do not harm my guest!" cried the older woman as she stood between the two and helped Liz to her feet.

Aphia Greene glared at the two women for a moment, then turned toward the horse, which had stopped at the end of the road just before the bridge. On her way to retrieve the steed, she turned once more to Liz.

""I know how hurt you were back then. Your tear-stained letter to Henry made me cry myself."

"Did he read that letter to you? I meant it to be personal, wanted him to know how I felt."

"No, he never saw that letter; never knew that you wished him a happy life with me. When my grandfather died, it was found folded up inside an old jacket that he wore every day."

"Henry never knew? I always thought he just ignored me.

There was no response."

"Miss, I kept that letter from my husband. Didn't want him to have anything at all to do with you for the rest of his life. He was mine forever." A tight grin spread across her face. "Ha! Ha! Mine forever? Ha! I should have realized that he would be as big a curse to my life as he was to yours."

She took the crumpled letter from her pocket and threw it on the ground in front of Liz, quickly strode to the horse, mounted, and rode away to the west on Sweden Road. A breeze caught the paper and blew it toward the mill pond. Hattie, who had emerged from the house during the commotion, ran after it.

"Stop, sister!" cried Liz. "Don't waste yourself chasing a worthless piece of trash. The woman who wrote that letter no longer exists. No one is interested in reading about her tears and rage."

81

Before leaving town, Liz and Hattie decided to drive by the house in which they were born. The steep ride up Mill Hill Road made the horse very tired, even when Liz decided to lighten the load by walking alongside the wagon. Now they sat on the chaise staring at a little cape on the corner of Deer Hill Road.

"The house looks so much better than I remember. When last I saw it," Liz mused, "Father had let it go nearly to ruins. Now it is painted and has a new roof."

A young boy who had been standing on the house porch when they stopped now waved and walked toward the road. Though the sisters were silent in their reveries, Hattie returned the wave.

"Remember that we must be on our way back to Bridgton," reminded Liz. "With all the time taken up with Aphia's tantrum, there is little left to visit with strangers, even if they do live in our house."

The lad walked up to a post-and-rail fence that stood just back from the road. He looked to be thirteen or fourteen years old. "Hello, ladies. Are you having a problem with your wagon?"

"No. We were just stopping to rest the horse and enjoy your view down to the pond. You live in a beautiful place," said Hattie.

"I know it, miss. This is the best place in Waterford to live. I have everything I want right here."

"What is your name, boy?" asked Liz.

"I am Lewis Keane, ma'am. This house is where my family lives now. Used to live in Harrison, but it's better here."

"You'd be wise to stay right here the rest of your life, Lewis Keane. The world doesn't have much more to offer than what is here in Waterford," said Hattie.

82

They drove down Mill Hill past the Wesleyan Chapel and back to the south on Waterford Road. Both seemed to be reminiscing and did not speak until they reached Bear Pond. Hattie broke the silence.

"When you think about it, not a lot of years have passed since we last were here. Yet so much has changed. I'm a mother of a lovely child, soon to be two children, with a kind and diligent husband who takes care of me. You are a successful seamstress with her own shop and many friends. Sometimes I think that we are living in a far different world than the one in which we had such a rough start. Yet this village has stayed much the same as it was."

"That is the same thought that was going through my mind. We have both been able to make good lives for ourselves. Our lives are different, but we should be proud. I am so pleased with what you have done to make such a wonderful family with Nathan."

"Yes, I am happy with my life, although there are things which I would like to change. Sometimes I wonder if I would be able to stand so strong on my own, as you have."

"And I wonder, dear sister, if I will ever be able to share the rewards you get from your family life."

Again there was silence between them until they approached North Bridgton, where they stopped to rest on the academy grounds. On a granite bench by a campus gate, they sat to enjoy the sandwiches Mrs. Hamlin had prepared for them. Liz began to share a part of her future plans that she had thus far been keeping secret from her sister and Beattie.

"You know that I have not been able to give myself to a man since Henry hurt me so. There have been several times I have tried, believe me. It's just that I have been guarding myself from having such a thing happen again. Now, however, I have a new relationship with the man who has been so supportive of me in Saco, Moses Webber. You've not met him, but trust me, he is a kind man much like Grandy and perhaps like your Nathan."

Hattie stared at her sister in disbelief. "Your boss? The man who hired you? Your business partner? Lizzie, isn't he an old man? What could you be thinking? You can't combine your business life with your private romantic life. Do you seriously believe this is a way to bring happiness into your life?"

"Sister, how can you judge me so harshly? You've not even met Moses. You don't know how kind he has been to me, how much he cares for me."

"Of course, you're right. I am sorry to react so. I only want happiness for you, but just think on it. Likely, at his age, he has been married before. If so, his family will look on you as no more than a gold digger who seeks his estate when he dies. His friends will think the same. What will Beattie think? You have not thought this out."

"Dear, you and I have been helpmates throughout this life. I ask you to trust me to have considered this relationship from all angles. While he and I are, first and foremost, partners in business, we have deep affection for each other. What I am doing is in the best interests of his family and mine. I will provide him with the companionship he has not known since his wife passed many years ago. He will, God willing, prove to be the companion and lover I have never known and a true friend as well."

"True friend, you say. Lover, you say. But these roles are not the same. Will you marry and both of you pledge devotion for as long as you live?"

Surprised at such a stern reaction, Liz rose from the bench, put on her pale yellow bonnet, and walked to the chaise. Hattie, perhaps realizing that she had been overly judgmental, slowly followed. Both climbed back to the seat. During the two-hour ride back to Bridgton, neither one said a word.

Arriving home in the late afternoon, they went into the house to find Beattie and the little one fast asleep on the parlor daybed. As they stood in the doorway looking at their family, Hattie reached out and touched her sister's shoulder. Neither wanted to disturb the sweet sleepers, so they tiptoed out to the kitchen.

"Liz, I am so sorry to have judged you so harshly. Surely you do have your own and your family's interests at heart. Please understand that the blessing of my children is also a blessed gift to you. They are part of your future as much as mine. I just do not want to see us all drawn back into the troubles of the past."

"Dear Little Sister, I cherish my family and would not hurt any of you in any way."

83

When Liz returned to Saco, she opened a new chapter in her life. She moved into the big Webber house and became the second Mrs. Webber—much to the chagrin of Moses's family, as Hattie had foretold. Her original plan had not necessarily included a formal marriage, but after the heated discussion with her sister, she decided that a legal union would be best.

Work on the boardinghouse conversion continued apace: opening day was to take place in early spring. It was 1891, and though the Pepperell was rapidly losing business to larger southern mills, demand for newer, more stylish styles would surely help keep both Webber's and Lizzie Millet's operations flourishing. During construction, Beattie was relocated to Bridgton to keep her from harm's way and to assist Hattie during the last months of her pregnancy. The new child was a healthy boy soon named Nathan, Jr. The birth was not easy for Hattie, but was not followed by the same problems as the first.

Mary and Maeve left Saco and moved to the third-floor apartment in Westbrook even though the first floor was still under construction. Maeve and Will, who now saw each other every day, began a relationship that would eventually lead to marriage and a large family. Mary became Liz's right-hand "man" and accepted the offer of a full partnership in the business, and the two women became almost inseparable during the times Liz was not in Saco.

Moses and Liz thrived in their relationship. He was a tender lover, just as he was a protector and supporter to her. She brought such happiness to his life that his family and friends gradually began to accept her. Over time, his health failed with age and diabetes, but until his death in 1910, life was good for the couple—both personal and business unions succeeded.

In September 1938, Lizzie Millet passed on. The cause of death was heart failure during her sleep. At the age of seventy-seven, she had lived a full life, had risen from a broken home to prove herself in the business world, and had enjoyed a happy family.

Epilogue

Hattie sat at the wheel of an emerald-green Chrysler Imperial that Nathan had purchased in 1933 at the end of his business career. She knew that it should have been sold following his death, but Nathan Jr. had convinced her to keep it. He said it was a safe car for her, but she thought he just wanted to be sure he was able to drive it around himself sometimes. As usual, the drive from her home in Bridgton had been a scary experience because she did not feel comfortable in such a powerful automobile. The Model A Ford they had owned before had been more to her liking.

She came to a stop in front of the big house her sister Lizzie had owned right up until her death. The place was currently vacant, with windows boarded up and weeds beginning to grow around its big front porch. A small hand-lettered sign still hung on a post above the mailbox: *MILLET'S AMERICAN DESIGNS,* it read.

Hattie had put this day off as long as possible; her older sister had been dead for over a year. Lizzie's cedar hope chest, sheathed in stamped tin with an ornate oriental pattern, still sat in the bedroom where she had spent the last of her days. At the funeral, Hattie, as next of kin, had volunteered to go through Liz's personal belongings to determine what might be of use to other family members and what could be donated to a church thrift shop. She had sorted out clothes, jewelry, books, and other belongings that had been in the closet, on the bedside table, or hanging on the walls. All these beautiful things had been acquired during the later years, when Liz had lived a happy personal life and was successful as a dressmaker.

The chest remained locked as it had been for many years. Hattie secretly hoped that the rusty old key would not work so that she would not have to handle all the reminders of loss and tragedy that were locked inside. Such mementos from their shared years of sadness and sorrow might better have been buried with the dead.

Reflecting on her sister's life, Hattie found it unfair that, even though the year was 1940, it was still, as it had been throughout her life, difficult for a woman to make her way on her own. If one, like Liz, wanted to succeed in a career or business, she would usually have to sacrifice many other things, such as a happy marriage, which thankfully had come to her sister later in life. The early difficulties back in Waterford and Bethel had somehow led the two girls in different directions: she to a more traditional life with Nathan and the kids, Liz to a creative life of career, recognition, and independence. Still, memories of the earlier shared difficulties always bound them together.

Hattie had long tried to avoid unlocking the chest and releasing the sleeping dragons therein. Now, with the house on the market, she had no choice but to complete her duty.

She pulled the car off busy Forest Avenue as far as she could, stepped out onto a soggy lawn, and climbed the wide steps. Inside the door, she stood for a moment taking in the emptiness of the place. All the furniture had been removed, as had pictures from the walls. The floor-length dark-green velveteen drapes were the only reminders left of Lizzie's artistic style of decoration. As she climbed the front stairs and entered a bedroom, empty except for a cushioned Morris chair and the tin-clad chest, her resolve to finish this particular family business waned. However, since the final accounting was her responsibility, she pulled the chair up to the chest, dutifully inserted the key, and unpacked the past.

By the time Hattie reached the bottom of the hope chest, remnants of Liz's life lay scattered about her on the floor. As each sad souvenir had been unearthed, dark memories weighed down on her heart. As she reached in for the last item, a pang of sorrow made her gasp and start to cry. It was the unfinished rose-pattern wedding dress, now sere and moth-eaten, the broken pattern paper still attached. As she unfolded the cloth, shreds of torn tissue stuck to her fingers.

Grief overcame the younger sister, herself now seventy-five years old. She cried at last for her departed sister—and for herself—as she held the unfinished dress on her lap and gazed into the depths of Lizzie's empty hope chest.